The Suitcase KID

Jacqueline Wilson

illustrated by
Ying-Hwa Hu

A Yearling Book

Published by
Dell Yearling
an imprint of
Random House Children's Books
a division of Random House, Inc.
1540 Broadway
New York, New York 10036

Visit us on the Web! www.randomhouse.com/kids

Educators and librarians, for a variety of teaching tools, visit us at
www.randomhouse.com/teachers

ISBN: 0-440-41371-0

Reprinted by arrangement with Delacorte Press

Printed in the United States of America

August 1998

10 9 8 7 6 5 4 3

OPM

In memory of Hilda Ellen Smeed

When my parents split up they didn't know what to do with me. My mom wanted me to go and live with her. My dad wanted me to go and live with him. I didn't want to go and live at my mom's new place or my dad's new place. I wanted to stay living in our *old* place, Mulberry Cottage, the three of us together. Four, counting my lucky mascot toy rabbit, Radish.

There were all these arguments about who would get custody of me. I thought they were talking about custard at first. I hate custard because you can never tell when there's going to be a lump and it sticks in your throat and makes you shudder.

1

My mom got mad and my dad got mad and I got mad too. I felt *I* was being split up. Half of me wanted to side with Mom. Half of me wanted to side with Dad. It was much easier for Radish. She just sided with me. She lives in my pocket so there's never been any hassle over who gets custody of her.

We had to go for family counseling. It seemed a bit stupid because my mom and dad didn't want to be a family anymore. This lady chatted to me. She was trying to be ever so casual but I knew she was trying to figure things out. She had some little dolls in her office, a mommy doll and a daddy doll and a whole set of children dolls in different sizes. She wanted me to play with them. I poked the mommy doll and the daddy doll in the stomachs and said I didn't like playing with silly old dolls.

But this lady saw me fiddling around in my pocket and she got a glimpse of Radish. I like to hold Radish tight when I'm feeling funny.

"Oh, what a dear little toy. Let me have a look," she said, in that silly voice grown-ups always use when they're trying to get you to like them.

"She's not a toy, she's a mascot," I said. I didn't want to show her Radish at all. She's mine and she's private. But I had to let this lady paw at her and undo her dress and turn her upside down in a very rude sort of way.

"What's Bunny's name?" she asked.

You'd have thought I was two years old, not ten. I just shrugged and shook my head.

"That's Radish," said Mom. "Andrea's had her for years and years. She's a very important member of our family."

"Actually, I bought Radish for Andrea. As a silly Saturday present. I like to give her a little treat every now and then," said Dad.

"You did not give Andrea Radish! *I* bought her one Christmas to go in Andrea's stocking," said Mom.

"Look, I can vividly remember buying that rabbit in the corner shop—"

"They don't even sell those sorts of toys at the corner shop. I bought it from the toy shop in town and—"

I snatched Radish back and put my hand gently over her ears. She can't stand to hear them arguing.

"Never mind," said the lady, trying to shut them up. She was still smiling at Radish.

"Hello, Radish," she said, peering right into her little furry face.

I scowled at her. Okay, Radish is real for me, but I can't stand it when grown-ups act like she's real too.

"I suppose you're feeling a bit sad and worried

about where you're going to live, little Radish," said the lady.

Radish kept her lips buttoned.

"We know what Mommy wants and we know what Daddy wants, but what do you want, Radish?" said the lady.

Radish wouldn't say a word.

"I think she's a bit shy," said the lady. "Maybe it's hard to say anything in front of Mommy and Daddy."

So she asked Mom and Dad to step outside the room for a few minutes. They didn't really want to. They both kept looking at me. You know what it's like at school when you're the team captain and everyone wants to be picked first to go in your team. Pick me, said Mom. Pick me, said Dad. I stared down at Radish until they'd gone outside.

"Poor Radish. This is a bit tough on her, isn't it," said the lady.

Radish and I stayed silent. The lady was quiet for a bit too. And Mom and Dad outside. I wondered if they were listening. But then they started up another argument. They whispered at first, but then got really mad and let it rip.

"Oh dear," said the lady. "Well, Radish. Here's Mommy. And here's Daddy." She propped these horrible dolls up at either end of her desk. Then she got some toy bricks and built a little house for the mommy doll and a little house for the daddy doll. She reached out and took Radish, putting her in the middle. Then she looked at me. "Where does Radish want to live, Andrea? Does she want to live in House A?" She pointed to the mommy doll's house. "Or does she want to live in House B?" She pointed to the daddy doll's house.

"She wants to live in House C. Mulberry Cottage, where we've always lived. With Mom and Dad and me," I said.

"I know she does. But she can't. Not anymore. It wouldn't work out. Just listen to Mom and Dad," she said. They were shouting now. "They can't be happy living together. You can see that for yourself, can't you, Andrea? But they both love you very much and they want you to be happy. So which house do you think you and Radish would be happiest in? House A?" She pointed to the mommy doll's house again. "Or House B?" Daddy doll's turn.

I looked at House A. I looked at House B. I looked at Radish. I made her walk one way. I made her walk the other. I made her hike backward and forward across the desk.

"She still wants to live in House C. But if she can't do that—and I still think she could—then she wants to live in House A *and* House B."

"Ah," said the lady. "You mean she wants to live in House A one week and House B the next week?"

So that's how it was decided. Radish lives with me, in my pocket, as she's always done. She's the luckiest one. And I get to live in my mom's house one week and my dad's house the next. It's as easy as ABC. Not.

is for Andy

My name is Andrea West but I mostly get called Andy. My sly little stepsister Katie calls me Andy Pandy. Everyone just thinks she's being cute. Katie specializes in cute. We are exactly the same age—in actual fact she's five days older than me—and yet she barely comes up to my waist. I happen to be big. Katie is extremely small. People don't guess she's ten. They think she's only about seven or eight, and she plays up to them for all she's worth. She blinks her blue beady eyes and wrinkles her small pink nose and puts on this squeaky little sugar-mouse voice. People all drool and practi-

7

cally nibble her ears. Katie is not a sugar-mouse. Katie is a King-Size Rat.

She's very spoiled. She's got her very own TV and VCR in her bedroom. When it's my week to sleep at my mom's place I have to share with Katie. She always insists that she gets to choose what's on TV, and she always gets first pick of the videos. She's got loads. She's got some pretty impressive creepy gory horror films that her dad knows nothing about. She hides them inside her Care Bears cases. She's also got the usual Walt Disney stuff. And then she's got this *Watch with Mother* video. Have you seen it? It's a bit dopey really, with little kids' programs that my mom and dad used to watch on TV a donkey's age ago. Including a little clown puppet called Andy Pandy. We watched it together, and that's when Katie started calling me Andy Pandy.

I couldn't stand it and I told her to shut up and she wouldn't. So I had to make her. My mom saw us pounding each other and she was furious. She didn't say a word to Katie. She just picked on me.

"How dare you hit Katie! I can't believe you could be so mean. You're twice poor Katie's size. I simply won't have this hateful bullying. You make me desperately ashamed of you. Katie's gone out of her way to welcome you into her home and then you behave like this!''

I wanted to hit my mom then as well as Katie.

"It's not fair. You don't know what she's like," I wailed, only I just sounded like a tattletale.

I stomped off and shut myself in the bathroom, Radish clutched tight in my hand. We stayed in the bathroom for ages and even when we came out we didn't speak to anyone all the rest of the day. Mom tried to make it up with me when we went to bed, but I still wasn't saying anything, not with Katie grinning away in the dark.

It wasn't until days afterward that Mom and I were on our own for once. Uncle Bill was working late. Only he's not my uncle. He's my horrible stepfather and I simply can't stand him. I can't understand what my mom sees in him. I take a good look and all I can see is this big hairy baboon. He's got all this thick black hair like a baboon. He's got a squished-up ugly face like a baboon. I've never caught a glimpse but I bet his butt's bright red like a baboon's too.

Paula was at her friend's house. Graham was shut up in his bedroom playing computer games. And Katie was out at her ballet class.

"So it's just you and me, pal," said Mom. "What shall we do, eh?"

I shrugged and made out I was busy watching TV. I was still feeling a bit miffed. But Mom came and sat beside me on the sofa and put her arm around me. I made myself go stiff at first but Mom went on cuddling and soon I sort of collapsed against her. I ended up on her lap. My mom's quite little and I'm big and I probably squashed her but she didn't seem to mind.

"Cheer up," said Mom, fiddling around with my hair, doing it in little tiny braids.

I'm growing my hair but it's taking forever. It hasn't even gotten near my shoulders yet. Katie has long hair all the way down her back and it's a glossy bright black.

"It's a very unusual combination," she told me smugly. "Blue eyes and black hair. I take after my mother."

Her voice always goes all sad and solemn when she talks about her mother. It's as if she died only last week and so you've got to feel sorry for her. In actual fact Katie's mother died when she was little and so she probably can't remember her much. Maybe she wouldn't even know her mom had blue eyes and black hair without the color photo in the silver frame on the windowsill.

My eyes are muddy brown. So is my hair. It's a bit depressing.

10

"I don't feel like cheering up," I said grumpily, though I didn't budge off Mom's lap.

"What was all the hoo-ha with Katie the other day?" said Mom.

"She called me names."

"What?"

"Andy Pandy."

Mom burst out laughing. "That's not too dreadful!"

"Yes it is," I said, and I shifted sideways, back onto the sofa.

"Andy Pandy. That's just a friendly nickname."

"It's after that TV program."

"Yes, I know. Well, Andy Pandy's okay. He's the hero. I suppose he's wimpy. Anyway, *you're* not wimpy. Why don't you call Katie Looby Lou and tease her a bit? But don't fight with her, I won't have that."

"You don't understand."

"Oh, moms never understand," said my mom, ruffling my hair. "Let's watch the show, eh?"

She turned the television up. I didn't bother explaining about Andy Pandy. He plays all these silly little games with Teddy and Looby Lou and then the lady with the silly voice says something.

"Time to go home."

And Andy has to get in his basket while she

sings the "Time to Go Home" song. Katie calls me Andy Pandy and she sings "Time to Go Home" in this sweet little voice but it's as if she's spitting at me. Because she knows I haven't got a home anymore.

is for Bathroom

We're all crammed in together when I'm at Albert Road. That's my un-Uncle Bill's house. I'm never going to call him Uncle. I don't even call him just plain Bill. Though he *is* plain. I don't call him anything at all. I don't even speak to him if I can help it.

I can't stand the way Mom talks to him. She snuggles up to him and hangs on his every word and roars with laughter at his stupid jokes. She doesn't even get grouchy if he goes out drinking with his buddies after work. That's really stupid, because she used to nag my dad like mad if he came home late.

Although that was probably when he was seeing that dopey Carrie . . .

My un-Uncle Bill is a painter and decorator, though you'd never think it if you saw his house. (That's how he and my mom met. When he came to paint our hall and stairs at Mulberry Cottage, because it was too high for Mom to reach. Bill the Baboon had a special set of scaffolding with planks. I'd like to make him walk his rotten plank. Right to the edge and over.) His own house on Albert Road is really scruffy, nowhere *near* as nice as Mulberry Cottage, so I can't see why my mom pretends she likes it here. She's starting to do the decorating herself, changing it all around. Making it her place.

There's nowhere that's *my* place, though. The others are always barging around the kitchen and the living room. My mom shares a bedroom with old Billy Baboon, so I'm certainly never going in there.

He's got three children: Paula, Graham and little ratbag Katie. I don't like any of them, but I suppose Paula's the best. She's fourteen and she doesn't think much of my mom and they keep having fights. I encourage this like mad, because then my mom might get fed up and want to leave. And then all I've got to do is get my dad to leave Carrie and we could all be a family again. We might even be able to buy

14

back Mulberry Cottage and start all over again, living happily ever after.

Paula has her own bedroom and she's got rock posters all around the room and she plays her stereo system so loudly that the whole house shakes. She's got special earphones but she deliberately doesn't use them. *We're* the ones who need earphones.

It's funny, Paula's so noisy, but Graham is the most silent boy you could ever imagine. He's twelve, but I'm much taller than him. If we had a fight I know I'd win, easy. But he's not the fighting sort. He's pale and twitchy with glasses and he just likes to shut himself up in his small bedroom and plug into his computer. I think he'll turn into a robot one day. He moves in this jerky sort of way, and the rare times he does speak his voice is flat like a machine.

Katie's got the biggest bedroom so she has to share it with me. It's not *my* fault. I don't want to share with her. I can't stand it. I can't ever dress up or practice making silly faces or play a good game with Radish because Katie's always there. I can't even get lost in a good book because Katie turns her TV all the way up or sings some silly song right in my ear to distract me.

So do you know where I go when I need a bit of peace and quiet? I lock myself in the bathroom.

There aren't any really good places to sit. The toilet gets a bit hard after a while. The edge of the bathtub is too cold. I wouldn't dream of sitting *in* the tub. I always just wash in the sink. The baboon has a bath every day and he leaves dark wisps of hair all over the place, and little crumbs of plaster and flakes of paint.

I collected some of his foul scummy hairs in a matchbox, together with a nail clipping and a shred of one of his dirty tissues. Then I concocted an evil spell and threw the box out the window. I waited hopefully all the next day for the news that he'd fallen off his ladder. But he didn't. Magic doesn't work. I should know that by now. I've wished enough times that Mom and Dad and I could be together again in Mulberry Cottage and it hasn't happened yet.

Even when I'm locked in the bathroom I can't always concentrate on my book. I used to read lots and lots and I got through every single story in the Book Box at school, and I went to the library too and I had my own collection of paperbacks, nearly fifty of them, some of them really big hard nearly grown-up books. But now my own books are shoved in a cardboard box somewhere and I can't get at them, and all the books from school and the library suddenly seem boring. I can't get into the stories. I just keep thinking about Mom and Dad and Mulberry Cottage.

So now I choose really babyish books to read, stuff I read years ago, when I was six or seven or eight. I can remember reading the stories the first time around and sometimes I can kid myself I'm little again, and everything's all right.

Sometimes it doesn't work, even in the bathroom by myself. So then I generally play a game with Radish.

She loves the bathroom. It's her favorite best-ever place. Don't forget she's only two inches tall. The sink and the bathtub are her very own swimming pool. I generally fix up a superslide by knotting Paula's pantyhose together and hanging them from the door hook to the bathtub faucet. Radish doesn't have a very slippery bottom so I soap her a lot to make her slide satisfactorily. This means Paula's pantyhose get a bit soapy too but that can't be helped.

Radish certainly doesn't like to swim in the baboon's hairy lair but she likes a quick dip in the sink, and she's getting very good at dives off the windowsill down into the water. Sometimes she turns somersaults as she goes.

When she starts to get shivery I dry her in the towel, and then she warms up using the sponge as her own trampoline. When she's tired of this she generally begs me to make her a snowman. I know this will get us into trouble but I don't care. I take the baboon's shaving cream and we make all the snowdrifts and then we start sculpting them into snow people. Last time I got a bit carried away. I made a snow girl and a snow rabbit and then I made a snow cottage. All right, it looked more like a big blob than a cottage, but the snow girl and the snow rabbit liked it a lot. I tried to do a tree too but the shaving cream went *phut* and I realized I'd used it all up. Nearly a whole can.

The baboon beat his chest and bellowed in the morning, but Radish and I didn't care.

is for Cottage

We didn't always live in Mulberry Cottage. We used to live in this crowded flat in the middle of London when I was very little. It was noisy and there was lots of trash everywhere and we kept getting robbed. Mom and Dad used to talk about moving to a pretty little cottage in the country but it was always just like a fairy tale.

Then one day we went for a ride in the car and it was very hot and I got bored and started whining and they got mad at me so I howled and wouldn't shut up and Dad stopped at a little corner shop to bribe me into silence. I stopped yelling and started happily slurping my way through an ice cream cone.

Mom and Dad had ice cream too, and we all went for a little walk in the sunshine. And that was when we saw it. The cottage at the end of the road. A white cottage with a gray slate roof and a black chimney and a bright butter-yellow front door. There were yellow roses and honeysuckle growing up a trellis around the door and the leaded windows, and lots of other flowers growing in the big garden. In the middle of the garden was an old twisted tree with big branches bent almost to the ground. Mom and Dad were so taken by the cottage that they'd stopped keeping an eye on me. I toddled through the gate and made for the tree because it was studded all over with soft dark fruit. I picked a berry and popped it in my mouth. It tasted sweet and sharp and sensational. My very first mulberry.

There was a For Sale sign on the fence. It seemed like we were meant to buy Mulberry Cottage. It wasn't quite in the country. It turned out to have a lot of dry rot and woodworm and for the first year there was dust everywhere and we couldn't use half the rooms. But it didn't matter. We'd found our fairy-tale cottage.

I found it. After all, I was the one who started yelling so they had to stop the car. It was my cottage. I was the one who called it Mulberry Cottage right from the start.

Mom made mulberry pies the first year we were there. And then she made mulberry jam. It didn't set properly but I didn't care. It was fun pouring your jam on your bread. I didn't mind a bit when it ran down my wrist and into my sleeve. I liked licking it off.

When Mom went back to work she stopped doing that sort of cooking. Dad tried making a pie once, but his pastry was all burned and crunchy. It didn't really matter, though, because the mulberries softened it up. He didn't try again so I just used to eat my mulberries raw.

Have you ever had a mulberry? They're better than raspberries or strawberries, I'm telling you. You have one mulberry and you want another and another and another. They stain quite a bit no matter how careful you are. You end up looking like Dracula with mulberry juice dripping bloodily down your chin, but who cares? You also often end up stuck in the bathroom with an upset tummy, but honestly, it's worth it.

My mouth is watering. I want a mulberry so much. I can't stand to think that there's someone else living in Mulberry Cottage now, picking my mulberries off my tree. There's someone else in my bedroom with the funny uneven wooden floorboards. I kept trying to pry them up hoping that someone in the past

21

would have hidden treasure underneath. And I was sure there was a secret passage because the walls were so old and thick. I know I'd have found the treasure and the passage if I could only have gone on living there.

is for Dad

Dad came to collect me on Friday evening. I got so excited and fidgety before he came that I couldn't even sit still to watch TV. I couldn't wait for him to get here—and yet when he tooted his car horn I suddenly clutched Mom and didn't want to go after all. It's always like that.

Dad doesn't come to the front door anymore. Dad and Mom still fight a lot if they're together for long. And once Dad and the baboon nearly had a fight. They both had their fists in the air and circled around each other. Mom yelled but they didn't take any notice of her. I kept tugging at Dad but he just brushed my hand away. It was Katie who stopped them from fighting.

"Oh, please stop, Daddy, you're scaring me," she squeaked, blinking the famous blue eyes.

I can't stand Katie.

There's one really good thing. My dad can't stand her either.

"I had another fight with Katie," I told Dad when we were driving over to his place.

"And who won?"

"*I* did."

Dad chuckled. "Good for you, Andy. She's a spoiled little brat if ever I saw one."

"Uncle Bill said I was spoiled the other day," I said.

I'd made a fuss because I didn't get the cream off the top of the milk for my cornflakes three days running. He said we all had to take turns. I said I never had to take turns in my old house with my mom and my dad. Uncle Bill said it was about time I learned to share. I said a whole lot of other stuff and I ended up getting severely told off. But I didn't care, because Paula let me have the top of the milk when it was her turn, because she says she's dieting.

"What nerve that man's got! I don't know what your mother sees in him," said Dad.

"Yes, he's horrible," I agreed happily.

"Is he horrible to you, Andy?" Dad asked, reaching out and giving my chin a little tickle.

"Well. Sort of."

"You tell me right away if he tells you off again or does anything else horrid, okay? Get on the phone right away. It's madness your having to live with them half the time. You'd be much happier with me, wouldn't you?"

"Mmm," I said, and I reached for Radish in my pocket.

"I miss you so much when you're at your mom's place," said Dad.

"I miss you too," I said.

When I'm with Mom, I miss Dad. When I'm with Dad, I miss Mom. Sometimes I can hardly believe that we all used to live at Mulberry Cottage together.

"Come here, sweetheart," said Dad, slowing down so he could give me a hug.

I cuddled up against his chest and he kept kissing the top of my head. I felt as if I was a juicy stretch of grass and he was a hungry sheep.

"My little girl," said Dad.

I love it when he calls me that. Even though I'm not little, I'm big.

He looked at his watch and gave me a squeeze.

"We're quite early, you know. Shall we go and have an ice cream soda together, just you and me?" He winked. "No need to tell Carrie."

Carrie is his new wife. She disapproves of anything that tastes really good, like ice cream sodas and hamburgers and fries and chocolate. She serves up the most horrible brown muck for our meals. She gives her children, Zen and Crystal, carrot sticks to eat instead of sweets. (They cheat, though. They're always swiping candy bars from the other kids in their kindergarten class.)

Ice cream sodas are my all-time favorites. I can never decide whether I like strawberry or chocolate best. My dad knows I always go back and forth between the two.

"How about two ice cream sodas today? One strawberry, one chocolate?" he suggested.

"Wow!" But I hesitated. Seeing he was in such a good mood . . . "Dad?" I said, trying to sound all sweet and sappy like Katie. "Hey, Dad, since we've got lots of time could we maybe do something else instead?"

"Instead of ice cream sodas? Gosh! Okay, pet, what do you want to do? Anything for my little girl."

I took a deep breath.

"Could we take a little drive and go and see Mulberry Cottage?"

Dad's arm went stiff. His face lost its smile.

"Oh, Andy. Don't start."

"Oh, Dad, please. I'm not starting anything. I just want to see Mulberry Cottage again, that's all."

"Why? There's no point. We're not ever going to be living in Mulberry Cottage again. There's another family living there now."

"I know. I just want to see it, that's all. Because I like it. And the mulberries should be out soon and we could maybe pick some and we could get Mom to make one of her pies and—"

"Don't be silly, Andrea," said Dad, and he started up the car and we drove off.

I didn't get to go to Mulberry Cottage. I didn't get a strawberry or a chocolate ice cream soda. It wasn't fair. It never is.

is for Ethel

For most of my life I was an only child. I didn't mind a bit. And then all of a sudden I got bombarded. I have five and a half stepbrothers and stepsisters.

There's Paula and Graham and horrible little Katie, who are my un-Uncle Bill's children. Then there are Zen and Crystal, Carrie's five-year-old twins. Yes, Zen and Crystal. Did you ever hear such dopey names? Mom fell down laughing when she heard.

And then there's the half. Carrie is going to have another baby.

I didn't figure things out for a bit. Carrie is very thin but she often wears long droopy smocky things so I didn't really notice her tummy. But then one Friday night when I was unpacking all my things I started up an argument with Zen. Crystal isn't too bad. She's got long fair hair and a little white face and she sucks her thumb a lot. Zen bites his nails. He's going to chew his fingers right down to the knuckle soon. He's got long fair hair and a little white face too. When I first saw them I thought they were twin girls. But though Zen looks like a little wimp he's as tough as old boots. He *wears* old boots, sort of miniature Doc Martens, and he packs a wallop with them too. There's a big poster about the Peace Movement in Carrie's kitchen but no one gets any peace at all when Zen's around.

He's got his old Teenage Mutant Ninja Turtles poster on his side of their bunk beds. Crystal's got one of a ballet dancer and she's started lessons herself and keeps twirling around in her pink satin ballet slippers. Carrie tried sending her to junior karate instead but Crystal hated it. Carrie tried to get Zen to go to ballet with Crystal but he just goofed off and was silly and the teacher complained. No wonder.

Anyway, I have to sleep in Zen and Crystal's bedroom every other week and it's a bore. They've got their bunk beds but otherwise it's not like a bedroom at all. Carrie lets them get all their toys out at once and they never have to put anything away. They have a tent in there too, and a weird fort made out of the clotheshorse, and lots of cardboard boxes that are supposed to be trains and shops and caves. You have to wade through all this junk to get across the room to the big cupboard. It's falling to pieces and half the drawers don't fit right, but Carrie's painted it with dragons and mermaids and unicorns and all sorts of other fairy-tale stuff so it looks quite pretty if you like that sort of thing.

I think I'd have maybe loved a cupboard like that when I was Crystal's age. I wouldn't mind one now. If I could have it back in my own bedroom at Mulberry Cottage.

Mom says it sounds as if I have to sleep in a garbage dump and she gets particularly annoyed that I don't have a real bed. Carrie's made this weird cotton sleeping bag that she says is like a Japanese futon. She embroidered little Japanese ladies and butterflies and birds all over the front and I thought it was especially for me and I couldn't help liking it a lot. But then I found out that Zen and Crystal's creepy little friends come to stay sometimes and they sleep in the Japanese bag too, so I went crazy.

I made a big fuss about my back hurting and my neck hurting and my everything else hurting after a night trussed up in the bag.

"Don't be such a whiner, Andy," Dad said sharply.

"Whiney-piney," said Zen, trampling on my feet in his boots.

"You can share my bunk bed with me if you want, Andy," said Crystal.

"No thanks. You wet the bed," I said.

"Only sometimes," said Crystal, blushing.

I felt a bit mean then. I wasn't really mad at Crystal. I was mad at Carrie because if my dad hadn't gone off with her I'm sure we'd all be living happily ever after in Mulberry Cottage.

I say lots of mean things to Carrie but she's never mean back. She always acts like she's pleased to see me but I'm sure she's not. She doesn't want me around half the time. She wants my dad to herself. I bet that's why she made the Japanese bed-bag. She can fold it up and stow it away in the cupboard. I bet she'd like to fold me up and stuff me out of sight too.

Anyway *again,* I was busy trying to clear a little bit of space for *my* stuff so I had to chuck some silly junky toys out of the way and Crystal didn't mind when her Barbie went whirling across the room and landed with her legs in the air and she just laughed when her My Little Ponies went flying through the air like Pegasus, but Zen started yelling that I was messing up all his Transformers and he started kicking me really hard. So I hooked my leg through his

31

and tripped him and he roared with rage and punched me right in the stomach.

"Stop it, Zen!" Crystal shouted. "You mustn't hit people in the stomach. Mom said."

"She said I mustn't hit *her* in the stomach, because she's going to have the new baby," said Zen. "I can still hit anyone else."

"Oh no you can't," I said, and I pushed him over and sat on him. "What's all this about a new baby?" I said, breathing hard.

"It's Mom and Simon's new baby," said Crystal.

She was sucking her thumb so it came out very indistinctly. I made her repeat it again, while I tried to catch hold of Zen's kicking legs.

"Stop that, Zen, you silly little squirt," I said, and I pulled his hair, which he hates.

He started yelling and Carrie and Dad came running and there was a bit of a fuss because I was the one on top of Zen, and I suppose I am twice his size.

"But he did kick Andy quite a bit," Crystal said fairly.

Maybe it's not so bad having Crystal for a stepsister. But I know one thing. I can't stand the thought of *another* one. One that will be my dad's little girl too.

"You're having a baby," I said fiercely to Carrie.

"That's right. Isn't it lovely?" said Carrie, smiling nervously.

"Why do you want more children when you've got Zen and Crystal?" I said.

"I want Simon's child too," said Carrie.

That made me feel sick. Dad was a bit red in the face too.

"We were going to tell you this weekend, honestly," he said.

"It's all right. I'm not really interested. I don't like babies," I said.

"Oh, come on. I think you'd like a baby sister," said Dad.

"No thanks. Anyway, you don't know it's going to be a girl. It could be a boy. A boy like Zen," I said.

My dad isn't crazy about Zen either. I'm glad. I don't see why Zen and Crystal get to have my dad all the time just because they haven't got one of their own. (Carrie said their dad couldn't face commitment. He probably took one look at Zen and made his getaway.)

"*Twin* Zens," I added triumphantly.

But Carrie shook her head.

"No. I had a sonogram. In case it was twins again. And it's just one baby. A little girl."

"Oh." I couldn't think of anything else to say.

There was this big long silence. Carrie looked at me. Then she looked at Dad. He didn't do anything. So Carrie came and put her arm around me.

"What shall we call your little sister, Andy?" she said.

Dad brightened up. "Yes, Andy. How about you choosing a name for her?"

Carrie looked a bit worried, but she nodded.

"Okay," I said. "I'll choose her name."

They're going to have to let me choose it now. They practically promised. And I'm going to pick the worst name ever.

I used to have this Great-great-auntie Ethel who smelled of pee and shouted at everyone. She took one look at me and said, "Who's that big gawky child with enormous feet? Let's hope she's got brains because she's certainly no beauty."

I've got brains all right. My little stepsister-to-be is going to be called *Ethel.*

is for Friends

Aileen was always my best friend right from the time we were in the first year at nursery school. Her mom and my mom were friends too and Aileen's mom would drive us all home after school. Sometimes we'd go back to Aileen's and her mom would make hot chocolate with marshmallows and Aileen and I would play with her Barbie dolls. Sometimes Aileen and her mom would come back to Mulberry Cottage with us and we'd have fruit juice—once we had *mulberry* juice—and Aileen and I would play with all my little toy animals.

Then we got old enough to do things without our moms and so we'd go to the park and play on the swings and we'd go down to the corner shop to buy potato chips and Coke and we'd crawl through a hole in the fence on this bit of wasteland and play games in the bushes.

We had such a great time. But now it's all different. When we left Mulberry Cottage, I couldn't go on playing with Aileen after school every day. My mom's new house with the baboon is miles and miles away. My dad's apartment with Carrie is even farther away in the opposite direction. Mom did let me have Aileen over for dinner one time, but Katie kept hanging around us and we didn't have anywhere private to play so we just ended up listening to Paula's records. We couldn't be secret and special the way we used to be.

I still see Aileen every day at school but it's not the same. Aileen's mom gives a lift home to Fiona now. Aileen and Fiona play together after school. We go around in this sort of threesome at playtime. Aileen keeps insisting she's still my friend but when we have to join up with a partner in class now she always goes with Fiona.

is for Garden

I come home from school by myself now. There isn't anyone to give me a lift. I have to walk down Seymore Road and through Larkspur Lane and up Victoria Street into town. I go to the bus station and then, when I'm staying with Mom, I get a 29 as far as The Cricketers pub and then I have a ten-minute walk. I have to get two buses when I'm at my dad's, a 62 and a 144, and then I have a fifteen-minute walk even after the two bus rides. I'm exhausted when I get back, I'm telling you.

I'd go crazy if I didn't have Radish to talk to on the way. Once or twice right at first I got lost and forgot the way and got that horrible hot swirly feeling in my stomach. I had to clutch Radish tight to stop myself from crying. Then I calmed down and asked a safe-looking lady with children to show me the way to the bus station.

Then another time my purse must have fallen out of my coat pocket because when I was lining up for the bus I went to get my money out and my purse was gone. I thought for a moment I'd lost Radish too but then I found her clinging to the pocket lining. She made me feel a bit better but I still didn't know what to do.

I could simply have told the bus driver I'd lost my purse but I was scared he'd get mad. He was one of those big fat men with a frowny face.

But I didn't have to ask him in the end because an old lady had been watching me frantically searching my pockets.

"What's up, dear? Lost your bus fare? Here, don't you fret, I'll pay your fare today."

I was very grateful and asked Mom for extra bus fare the next day to pay her back. Mom got ever so upset when she found out what had happened.

"Poor old Andy. You must have been so worried. Oh dear, I do hate it that you have to come home by yourself now."

Mom can't come and meet me because she works nine to five in a drugstore now to help pay the bills. I wish she'd chosen a more exciting store like a bakery or a toy shop or a pet shop. You can't get very excited when she brings home half-price toilet paper rolls and stale cough drops.

"*I've* been coming home from school by myself since I was six years old, Auntie Carol," said Katie smugly.

"That doesn't count. Your stupid old school is just down the road. A baby of six months could crawl to it," I said.

"I wish you'd switch to Katie's school, Andy," said Mom. "It would be so much more sensible."

"But if I went to Katie's school then it would take me hours and hours to get there when I'm staying at Dad's," I said.

"Well. All this to-ing and fro-ing is getting ridiculous anyway," said Mom. "You're getting worn out, Andy. I'm thinking about you, darling. It would be so much better if you settled down in one place for a while and went to the local school."

"That's what Dad says. He wants me to settle down with him. And go to Zen and Crystal's school," I said.

I'm not going to go to any other old school. I like *my* school. Even though it isn't really the same anymore. Aileen isn't the same. The teachers aren't even the same. They made a bit of a fuss over me at first when Mom and Dad split up but now they often get mad at me. I forget to do things or I lose my books or I don't listen in class.

"If you'd only try to *concentrate,* Andrea," they say.

I am concentrating, but it's not often on class nowadays.

There's only one good thing about all these boring journeys to and from school. I've discovered another mulberry tree. It's in a garden on Larkspur Lane so I get to see it whether I'm living at my mom's or living at my dad's. It's not as nice as our mulberry tree at Mulberry Cottage, of course. It's very old and gnarled and bent over, but it still grows lots of mulberries.

I watched them ripening from red to purple to bright black and brimming with juice. No one seemed to be picking them. The grass grew lavishly and the flowers were in tangled clumps and the creepers were crawling all over everywhere. Perhaps no one was living there anymore.

I peered over the high fence every day, trying to see the house, though it was hidden by another tree. I never heard a radio or saw a lawn chair out in the garden. I started to lean right over the gate, peering in. Sometimes I got Radish out so she could peer too.

The garden would be fairyland for Radish. She

40

could hike through the grass playing Jungle Explorers, swinging on the creepers like a tiny Tarzan. And she could eat mulberries . . .

My mouth watered as I looked at those great big berries. One day I couldn't stand it any longer. I got my leg up over the gate, I jumped down into the garden, I ran through the long grass, I reached the mulberry tree, I snatched a handful of berries and then rushed back. I scratched my hand on the tree and banged my shin badly climbing back over the gate but I had the mulberries safe in my hand. I crammed them into my mouth and the juice spurted over my tongue and I closed my eyes because it was just just just like being back at Mulberry Cottage.

I still stop at the mulberry garden every day. And mostly I slip inside.

is for Haiku

*I wish I was
in Mulberry Cottage
with Mom and Dad
and Radish.*

That's a haiku. We did haiku in English. When the teacher said we were going to learn about haiku we all got excited because we thought it was going to be like kung fu. But haiku are little Japanese poems. She read us some and there was one about a garden in the moonlight with a willow and wild berries. I started really listening. I decided I liked haiku a lot.

In my dreams
I am as small as my rabbit
and I am safe
at home.

That's another haiku.

I live with Mom
I live with Dad
I live with Radish
Can't we join up?

And another.

is for Ill

I always seem to be getting ill nowadays. I get these headaches or sometimes they're tummy-aches or other times it's an ache all over and I'm either much too hot or so cold I'm shivering. It's always worse on Fridays. That's changeover day.

A few Fridays ago I had a bit of a sniffle on Friday morning. I burrowed under the bedcovers till I got boiling hot and sweaty and then I called Mom, sounding all sad and sore and pathetic.

Mom felt my forehead and gave me a worried hug. I knew Katie would tease me later about being a baby but I didn't care. Mom always makes far more fuss over me on Fridays. I clung to her and said I felt really lousy.

"I think you've got the flu," said Mom. "Oh dear. Well, you certainly can't make that awful trip to school, not in this state. You'd better stay in bed."

"All by myself?" I said, hunching up as small as I could.

Mom hesitated. "Maybe I'd better stay home from work."

"Oh, Mom, would you?" I said.

"They won't like it. But it can't be helped. You're really not at all well, dear. You'd better stay in bed all weekend."

"What, at Dad's?"

"No, you'll have to stay put here. You're not up to traveling," said Mom firmly.

I started to feel really sick then. I wanted to stay with Mom and have her making a big fuss over me— but I still wanted to go to Dad's too.

But I made the most of that Friday all the same. Katie flounced off, forbidding me in a whisper to touch any of her videos or records—"Or I'll get you later."

I can beat her in a straight fight but she's got all sorts of devious hateful ways of hurting me. She hides my stuff. She scribbles inside my schoolbooks.

45

Once I found poor Radish floating miserably in the toilet and I just know Katie threw her there. Radish had to spend the night in a bowl of disinfectant and she didn't lose the smell for days and days, so that whenever I hugged her close my eyes stung.

But I didn't need to play Katie's records or videos or touch any of her boring junk. Mom came and sat on the edge of my bed and she read the paper and I read one of my old baby books and then when I started to act low Mom read some more books aloud to me. She fixed me a lovely lunch, tomato soup and a soft white roll, and then she made me a special bowl of green Jell-O. She even let me pretend it was lettuce-flavored so that Radish could wade through this wonderland and get her paws all sticky.

We all had a nap after lunch and when I woke up Mom lent me her white lace hankie and I played Brides with Radish. I said I was starting to feel a lot better and suggested I could get up, but Mom wouldn't hear of it. And then the others came home from school and the baboon came back from his work and then about seven o'clock I heard the car toot outside. It was Dad coming to pick me up.

I tried jumping out of bed then but Mom hauled me right back. She went to speak to Dad. Only they didn't do much speaking. They were shouting in less than a minute. Then Dad stormed right into the house and up the stairs to see me. Un-Uncle Bill said he had no right to come barging in and Dad said he had every right if his daughter was ill. Dad gave me a great big hug but then he held me at arm's length and looked at me.

"You seem fine to me. Maybe you've got a cold, but everyone's got the sniffles just now. Come on, Andy, get dressed and we'll get cracking," said Dad.

I started to do as I was told, but Mom started shouting that it would be madness taking me out into the cold air when I had the flu and that I was to get back into bed this instant.

I stood in my pajamas shivering in the middle of Katie's bedroom, not knowing what to do. Mom won that battle in the end. Dad stormed out and I was so scared he was blaming me that I started crying. Mom bundled me back into bed, insisting that it was wicked for Dad to get me in such a state.

I had to stay in bed most of that weekend and it stopped being a treat and started to get really boring. I didn't have Mom to myself because all the others were around. And then on Sunday Katie insisted she'd caught my flu and she stayed in bed too. She didn't want my mom nursing her. She just wanted her dad.

So the baboon sat her on his lap and called her his poor little princess and other sickening stuff. He ran

47

out to the convenience store at lunchtime and bought her a huge box of chocolates. Katie wouldn't eat any of Mom's chicken and roast potatoes and peas but she hogged almost that whole box of chocolates to herself.

I hated seeing her all cuddled up with the baboon. It made me miss my dad even more. I couldn't wait till the next Friday so I could see him again. But then he was all huffy with me for ages, acting like it was my fault I'd stayed on at Mom's.

"You can't kid me, Andy. You were playacting," he said angrily, and when I tried to get on his lap he tipped me off and said I was behaving like a big baby.

He was a bit nicer on Saturday and by Sunday he was okay and he played cards with me and one evening that week he came home early from work and took me out and bought me an ice cream soda . . . but it still wasn't as good a visit as usual.

Maybe I'd better not get ill again for a while.

is for Jell-O

I was ill the very next time I went to Dad's. Not just a little sniffle. I felt a bit shivery and strange on Thursday, but then I generally do at Carrie's house. She has the basement apartment and it's always got this sour damp smell even though she burns incense sticks all day long. She's got storage heaters. I don't know what they store but it's certainly not heat. I wear a thick sweater even in the summer and by the autumn I wear two of everything, even two pairs of underwear.

Carrie doesn't seem to feel the cold herself and

floats around in her filmy smocks without a shiver. Zen and Crystal are the same. They wander around stark naked after a bath or play for hours in their pajamas while I hop around in the Japanese bag absolutely frozen.

I told Dad I felt funny but he didn't take much notice. Carrie tried to put her arm around me to give me a hug.

"It's Friday tomorrow, isn't it. Poor old Andy."

I wriggled away from her. I don't like her holding me at the best of times. I especially can't stand it now, when she's got this big tummy full of the baby sticking out in front. Zen and Crystal put their hands on her tummy and giggle when they feel the baby moving. It gives me the creeps.

I kept dreaming about the new baby that night. Carrie's tummy swelled and swelled until she got as big as a whale and couldn't even waddle around anymore. And then the baby was born and it was huge too, even taller than me, with a great big lolling head and beady blue eyes that glared balefully at me. It bawled whenever I got near it so Dad said I'd better keep out of the way. It went on yelling even when I was in the bathroom so Dad said I had to go all the way out to the freezing cold garden.

I started yelling too then, and Dad got really mad

and said I wasn't setting my little sister Andrea a good example.

"What do you mean, Andrea? *I'm* Andrea. The new baby can't be called Andrea too. I've got to give her a name, you said I could. She's Ethel. I'm calling her Ethel."

The baby roared and Dad pushed me right out into the road.

"Don't be so silly. You're not Andrea. My baby's my little girl and she's called Andrea," Dad shouted from the house, struggling with the giant baby.

"*I'm* your little girl! I'm Andy!" I screamed as I dodged in and out of the traffic.

Then a car hit me hard in the chest and I opened my eyes and there was Zen sitting on top of me.

"Wake up, Andy!" he said, jiggling up and down.

"You were shouting, Andy," Crystal said, bending over me, her long hair tickling my face. "Were you having a bad dream?"

"Mmm. Get off me, Zen," I said. My voice came out in a weird croak. It hurt a lot. I wasn't shivery anymore. I was boiling hot.

"Get *off* her, Zen," said Crystal, pushing him. "I don't think you're very well, Andy."

"I don't think I am either," I said, and I started to cry.

"I'll get Mom," said Crystal.

"No, get my dad," I croaked.

They both came. Carrie sat cross-legged beside me, her tummy huge under her nightie. She sighed sympathetically.

"Poor little sweetie pie, Friday always makes you feel bad, doesn't it," she said. "Would you like me to show you the relaxation exercise I do at my child-birth class? It really helps you stop feeling tense."

"She's not feeling tense, she really is ill," said Dad, his hand on my forehead. "She's got a fever—feel, Carrie."

I squirmed away from Carrie's cool fingers and clutched at Dad.

"My throat hurts. And my head. And my neck and my arms and my legs. Everywhere hurts. Oh, Dad, will you stay home from work and look after me?" I begged.

"My poor little darling. Yes, you've got a nasty sore throat. All right, no school. But Carrie will look after you."

"I want you, Dad."

"Now you're being silly," said Dad, but he didn't sound mad. He ruffled my hair and hugged me close. And to my amazement he phoned his office after breakfast and told them he was taking a day's leave.

"I can't help it if it's not convenient," he said. "My little girl needs me."

I was really glad I had a sore throat then, even though it hurt so much. Dad tucked me into his and Carrie's bed, making a special nest for me, and then we played paper games all morning, tic-tac-toe and Hangman and Battleships. We haven't been able to play paper games properly for ages because Zen and Crystal are always around and they're too little to play and they just scribble and waste the paper.

Carrie made this bean casserole thing for lunch but the only sort of beans I like are baked beans out of a can so I wouldn't eat any.

"My throat's too sore," I said, making it croak a little more.

"Oh dear," said Carrie, looking sad. "Isn't there anything I can get you, Andy? What would you really like?"

"Jell-O."

"Jell-O. Right. I'll make you a lovely fruit gelatin for dinner," said Carrie.

She went out and bought some oranges specially, and spent ages in the kitchen.

"I've never made a gelatin before but I *think* it's going to turn out all right," she said.

"It's easy to make Jell-O, you just pour on boiling water and stir," I said.

"Oh, that's Jell-O out of a package," said Carrie, looking shocked. "I'd never give you junk food, Andy. You need natural fresh food with lots of nourishment."

Carrie's gelatin didn't look very nourishing when she brought me a plate at dinnertime. It was supposed to be orange gelatin but it wasn't orange-colored. It was a weird sickly brown. It wasn't like Jell-O either. It didn't stick. It sort of slid around the plate. Radish was quivering in my hand, ready for another glorious Jell-O feast, but when she saw it for herself she jumped back into my pajama pocket, her ears drooping.

"Come on, Andy, eat up your nice gelatin," said Dad. "Isn't Carrie kind to make it for you specially?"

"I'm not really hungry now."

"Don't be silly, Andy. You've got to eat something."

"I feel sick."

"Now, don't start."

But I did feel sick, and it wasn't just because of the gelatin. Mom was due to come and collect me and I knew there was going to be trouble.

I lay waiting. I heard my un-Uncle Bill's van draw up outside. I heard Mom's footsteps and the tap on the steps down to the basement apartment. I heard the door knocker. And then I heard the quarrel.

54

"What do you *mean*, Andrea's in bed? My God, I simply can't believe this! I didn't think even you could stoop so low! Just because Andrea was genuinely ill the other weekend . . . Oh, of course she's not ill this time! You're just being deliberately obstructive, trying to get your own back in as nasty and spiteful a way as possible . . . It's just typical! Come on, hand Andrea over this minute."

"The child is very ill. She has a sore throat, and a fever—"

"Well, I'm not surprised, stuck in this damp old apartment. It's disgraceful, no place for young children—"

"Well, if you hadn't bled me dry over the divorce we could afford a better place—"

"Oh, don't give me that rubbish. And you don't even make sure Andy has a proper bed. She's told me about having to sleep on the floor. I can't believe it, you're too cheap to buy a real bed for your own little girl—and yet *her* kids have got bunk beds, I know. Well, if Andy really *is* ill then I insist she comes home with me where I can nurse her properly. Andrea? Andrea, where are you, darling? It's Mommy. I've come to take you home with me."

I heard her blundering around the apartment for quite a while before she got the right room.

"You poor little lamb!" she said, rushing to me.

55

"Why have they stuck you in here? Ugh, in their bed. Come on, let's put your coat on over your pajamas. You're coming home with me this instant."

I jumped out of bed obediently and stepped straight into the plate of gelatin. I stood shivering, up to my ankles in brown slime.

"Oh my God! *What's that?*" Mom screeched.

"It's Jell-O. Carrie made it for me."

"Jell-O?" snorted Mom. "That stupid hippie's been feeding you that muck and calling it *Jell-O?*"

"Will you quit calling Carrie names?" Dad roared.

"I'll call her anything I like, the dirty slut! She's not looking after my daughter again, do you hear me? I'll send the social services around. You're stupid enough to take on her hippie twins and she looks as if she's about to have your baby any minute, but I'm telling you one thing—she's not looking after *my* daughter, not anymore."

is for Katie

Mom took me home with her and said I wasn't ever going to go back to Dad's. Dad called up and came around and sent furious letters. I stayed in bed with my sore throat and tried to forget about them both. I played lots of Under-the-Bedcovers games with Radish. She had a sore throat too and we knew the only possible cure would be a sip of magical mulberry juice so we searched high and low across the dark and barren land (you try crawling around under your bedcovers) but our throats remained sorely parched.

"What are you doing under there, you stupid jerk?"

It was Katie, back from school.

"How's the poor little invalid now?" she said nastily. "When are you going to shove off back to your boring old dad, eh? I'm getting sick of you cluttering up my bedroom. Your mom's not *serious*, is she? You're not going to be here always?"

I emerged red-faced from under the covers.

"I don't know," I mumbled.

Katie slotted a video into place and pressed the button. A horribly familiar little puppet wobbled into view.

"Oh ha ha, very funny," I said.

Katie played the fast forward so Andy Pandy and Teddy jerked about like crazies and then stopped the tape the moment she spotted the basket.

"Time to get into your basket, Andy," Katie said, in the lady's silly high-pitched tone. "Did you get that, Andy Pandy? Fold up your big huge horrible arms and legs and stuff your fat head into your basket, right? I'll mail you off to your dad. Only once the new baby's born they won't have room for you there either so you'll just have to stay stuffed up in your basket forever, okay, because nobody wants you."

I clutched Radish tightly. I knew Katie was just winding me up deliberately. But it was working. I *felt* wound up. Tied up so tight I could hardly breathe.

"They do so want me," I croaked. "My mom wants me. My dad wants me. That's what all the fuss is about now. They both want me so much."

"Oh no they don't," said Katie. "They only go on about you because they want to get at each other. If they really truly wanted you then they'd have stayed in that boring old cottage you keep going on about. But your dad left and your mom left. Your dad wants his new lady. Your mom wants my dad. They want them, not you."

"Shut *up*!" I said, and I reached out of bed and tried to hit her.

It was just a flabby punch, it couldn't have hurt her at all, but she immediately started squealing and Mom came running.

"Whatever's the matter now?" Mom shouted above the racket, taking hold of Katie.

"Andy's poked my eye out and it *hurts*!" Katie roared.

"Andrea! I thought I'd put a stop to this nonsense! I won't have you bullying poor little Katie. Come here, Katie, let's see. Of course your eye's all right. Although, oh dear, yes, it is a bit red. Andrea, how *could* you?"

"I didn't touch her silly old eye," I protested truthfully. But then I looked at my fist. Radish's ears were sticking out of it. It looked as if Radish had done the poking for me.

I tried to explain but Mom wouldn't listen. She was very very mad. Then the baboon came home and I eavesdropped anxiously and she told him. And Katie started crying all over again just so that he would make a fuss over her. Then he came into the bedroom to see me and I got really scared.

I decided to poke his eye too if he shouted or smacked me. He had no right to tell me off. He wasn't my dad. I suddenly badly wanted my own dad and burst into tears.

"Yes, well, I'm glad to see you're feeling sorry, Andrea," he said. "Dear oh dear, you little girls! And I thought it would be great for you both, being the same age and all that. But listen to me, Andrea. I know you've had a hard time and you're not very well just now but that still isn't really any excuse. You must stop hitting Katie or you'll really hurt her. She's small and she's not used to such roughhousing. Her poor old eye is very sore. It could have been really nasty, you know. I don't want my baby to end up getting badly hurt. She's been a good little girl, sharing her bedroom and all her precious things with you. So I'd like you to try to be a bit grateful, Andrea. I know you're a nice little girl underneath even though you've got a quick temper. You've inherited that from your dad, obviously. But you've got to learn to control yourself, dear.''

I had the greatest difficulty controlling myself right that minute. I wanted to scream and kick and hit and rage because it wasn't fair. Katie always hurts me far more than I can hurt her. And I don't want to share her horrid bedroom. I want my *own* bedroom, back in Mulberry Cottage. My own place with my own things where I can be with my own rabbit.

is for Lake

The garden on Larkspur Lane has a lake! Well, not a real lake. It's really a round brick goldfish pond—but it's a magnificent lake for Radish.

We go there nearly every day after school, even though the mulberries are finished now. We've started to explore the garden thoroughly. Once we thought we saw a face at the window and we had to run like mad. We didn't go back for several days, walking quickly past the gate without even looking in, but we missed the garden badly.

Radish jumped over the gate by herself so I had to go after her. I wanted to stay close to the mulberry tree, but Radish found a crazy-paved path and followed it around a corner behind a hedge and there were three mossy steps down into another garden. The lawn was long and lush there too, right up past Radish's ears, and if I crouched down at her level I couldn't see the lake until we were right on top of it.

I don't think I've ever seen Radish so excited. She loves her dips and diving sessions in the bathroom at Mom's place (there's no real lock on the door at Dad's and there's a gap under the bathtub where the spiders live so Radish doesn't like playing there) but the lake was pure paradise by comparison.

She wanted to wade in right away, but I kept her paddling cautiously at the edge in case it got too deep. We both got a shock when an orange whale suddenly rose up out of the water and nibbled Radish's paws. I snatched Radish out of the way. We've learned the story of Jonah and the Whale at school and I didn't like the idea of gutting a goldfish to retrieve my Radish. But she didn't seem too bothered by the fish. I looked very carefully at their mouths. They just opened and shut as if they were blowing harmless kisses. They didn't seem to have *teeth*. Still, maybe they could suck at Radish and then swallow her whole.

I decided Radish had better go boating. I found various big leaves but as soon as I stood her on board the leaves started sinking. I tried collecting twigs but I needed something to stick them all together. I swiped some Scotch tape from the kitchen drawer at Mom's place and stuck the twigs together the next day and made quite a good little raft but Radish didn't seem too happy on it. It tipped too much. I was scared she'd sail right into the middle of the lake and then slide in under the water, out of her depth.

She needed a real boat, not a raft.

I sidled up to Graham after dinner the next day.

"Hey, Graham," I said, smiling at him.

He blinked a bit behind his glasses. We've barely spoken to each other ever since my mom's lived at his place. He generally makes himself scarce in his room with his computer. He's clever and gets a lot of extra homework. The baboon calls him the Boy Wonder. I don't like the way he says it. He doesn't seem to think that much of Graham. He's crazy about Katie and he cares a lot about Paula too, though he's always nagging at her for wearing too much makeup and staying out late. But he often makes these snide remarks about Graham. Graham doesn't say anything back. Graham hardly ever says anything very much.

"Graham, you haven't got a toy boat, have you? I mean, I know you're too old for toys now, but did you use to have one?"

Graham shook his head. "I made myself one with an old model set once."

"Did you? Did it float okay?"

"No, it's metal, so it wouldn't float."

"Well then, it was a pretty stupid boat, wasn't it?" I said, disappointed. "What does float, Graham? I've tried wood, but it's not right."

"Cork."

"Cork. What's that? Oh, I know, like in the top of a bottle. But it wouldn't be big enough. What else floats?"

"Rubber."

I shook my head, thinking about the eraser in my pencil case.

"Still too small. Come on, Graham, what else?"

"Plastic."

I thought hard. I went back to the living room. I borrowed one of the baboon's tapes, making sure no one was looking. I tried floating the plastic case in the bathtub. It did okay, but as soon as I tried to launch Radish on it they both sank. It needed to be bigger. A video case. Aha.

The next day after school Radish sailed the good ship *Video* from one side of the lake to the other. She had the sail up and stood on the sundeck, her black eyes bright with bliss.

is for Mr. Magic

om still said I couldn't go back to Dad's.
Dad called his lawyer. We had to have another family counseling session. It was the same lady, the one with the mommy doll and the daddy doll and the bricks to make House A and House B.

"Hello, Andrea. How's Radish?" she said.

I just shrugged, but I was impressed that she'd actually remembered Radish's name.

Mom and Dad ranted on and on. I didn't say much at all. Neither did Radish. The lady kept looking in my direction and asking me what we thought. We shrugged so often our shoulders ached.

It was fun hearing Mom trashing Carrie and Zen and Crystal and it was fun hearing Dad trashing the baboon and Paula and Graham and Katie but it was no fun at all hearing them trashing each other. I started to get my sore throat back, and I felt sick and I had a pain in my tummy. I went off to the rest room down the corridor to see if that might help the pain. I crept back and listened for a bit outside the door.

"How do you think Andrea's coping with all this?" said the lady.

"It's awful for the poor little lamb," said Mom.

"Yes, it's really unsettling her," said Dad. "Though when she's been with me a few days she calms down—and by the end of the week she's almost her old happy self."

"That's because she knows she can come back to me soon."

"That's absolute rubbish! The poor kid's been missing me dreadfully, she says so herself."

"Have there been any behavior problems at all?" asked the lady.

I tensed a little.

"She's always fine with me."

"We get on like a house on fire, always have."

"It's just that the school says she's rather withdrawn and isn't doing very well in her classwork."

67

"What do you mean, withdrawn? She's always been very outgoing and she's got tons of friends."

"And she's extremely bright, nearly always at the top of the class."

"Yes, of course, but she has had quite a lot to cope with recently."

I nodded bitterly behind the door.

"Children in these circumstances often develop worrisome little habits that show they're under stress. They get whiny and demanding. They bite their nails. They often wet the bed."

"The nerve!" I whispered. "I do *not* wet my rotten old beds."

"Sometimes they start stealing, but it's not as serious as it sounds. It's simply a way of looking for affection, taking a few goodies because they feel very badly treated."

"Oh dear," said Mom, her voice catching. "You see, the thing is, Andrea has started taking a few things recently."

"What?" I whispered. "I haven't! I'm not a thief! What are you *talking* about, Mom?"

"Well, Andrea's never stolen anything when she's with me. So it just shows she wants her dad."

"It's not really stealing. And she takes such silly things. Things she can't possibly want. It's not as if she helps herself to money or chocolates or anything

68

like that," said Mom, sounding nearly in tears. "I haven't said anything to her, but I've been getting really worried. It started off with her taking my Scotch tape. And then she took one of Bill's cassettes. I knew she doesn't like his music so I thought she was just trying to be annoying. But then she took Katie's video case. That's what's really puzzled us. She doesn't like that video, the *Watch with Mother* one; the Andy Pandy puppet gets on her nerves. But she didn't take the video, just the *case*. What in the world would she want the case for? It doesn't make sense."

I stuck my tongue out at the door. It made perfect sense.

"Perhaps she just wanted to annoy Katie?" said the lady.

"Perhaps," said Mom. "She certainly doesn't get along with her. They're always fighting."

"She fights a lot with Zen and Crystal too," said Dad, "but if only Andrea could be with us for longer, I'm sure she'd put down roots and we'd be like one big happy family, especially when the new baby's here."

"She needs to be with me," said Mom. "She can't cope with the idea of a new stepsister; she's talked about it to me."

"Yet she's already having to cope with five ready-made siblings," said the lady. "You can't expect Andrea to get along with them. She doesn't want to be with them, she doesn't want to be with your new partners—she simply wants to be with you two."

I nod, clutching Radish.

"And of course that's not possible."

It *is.*

"I wonder where Andrea's gotten to? I'd better go and look for her."

I take my cue and go back into the room. They all three give me big false smiles. I don't smile back. I still don't say anything. They think they've figured me out but they know nothing. And they're wrong about my new brothers and sisters, as a matter of fact. I don't think much of Zen but Crystal's okay, she can be quite sweet sometimes. I detest and despise little sugar-mouse Katie but Paula's funny, though she gets miffed at me when I use her drying pantyhose as a slide for Radish. But the best one of all is Graham. We are now friends.

He kept out of the way as usual for a few days and then he suddenly waylaid me on the stairs.

"I've got something in my room for you," he muttered.

It was a boat. He'd made me a real little Radish-size boat out of pieces of wood carefully nailed together and then painted. There's a real sail made from an old hankie and a little red ribbon flag on top.

"This one floats," said Graham. "I've tried it out in the bathtub. And it'll take one passenger easily."

"Oh, Graham! You're Mr. Magic!" I gave him a big hug. He turned very pink and his glasses misted over. "It's a lovely boat. It must have taken you ages. Why did you do it for me?"

"Because I like the way you keep bashing Katie," said Graham, grinning. "I can't stand her either. She always used to pester me and tease me and mess up my stuff. Now she leaves me alone because she's got you to plague."

"Yeah, it's not fair. And I can't ever get away from her." I considered, my head on one side. "It's awful sharing a room with her. Tell you what, Graham, I could come in here with you sometimes, couldn't I?"

"Oh, th-this is too small for two people, what with my computer and everything," Graham stammered, blinking anxiously.

"It's okay. I've got my own secret place where I go, actually."

"The bathroom?"

"No, much much better than the bathroom. I go there after school. That's where I'll sail my boat.

Thanks ever so much, Graham. Here, we're friends now, aren't we, you and me?"

"Yes, okay, if you like," said Graham.

I do like. And so does Radish. She liked the video vessel very much but she *adores* her real sailing boat. She'd sail the lake all day long if I let her.

is for Night

Katie keeps me awake half the night. She won't have the light out, for starters. Well, she'll switch the main light off but she's got this little china lamp in the shape of a toadstool with all these dinky rabbits and squirrels perched on little china chairs inside (Radish squeezed through the little door and tried to make friends but they didn't want to). The lamp glows all night long, and then Katie has her own flashlight and she nearly always has her television on too. She turns the sound down low but the picture goes on flickering.

The only way I can find any real dark is under the covers and then I nearly suffocate.

"Switch that stupid set *off*!"

"It's my TV. It's my bedroom. I can do what I want."

"I'll tell my mom."

"I'll tell my dad."

"I want to go to sleep."

"Well, *I* want to stay awake."

"Look, I'm turning it off, so tough toenails," I said, jumping out of bed and switching off the set.

"And *I'm* turning it on, so tough toenails twice," said Katie, bouncing out of bed and switching it right back on.

She likes it when we have these long arguments late at night. She likes to stay wide awake. Sometimes I have a bad dream and I wake up at two or three in the morning and if I look over at Katie's bed her eyes are nearly always open, big and blue and unblinking.

It's not that she can't go to sleep. She fights terribly hard not to. She almost never lies down comfortably. She sits up with all her pillows propped behind her. She eats cookies and drinks a lot of water so she has to keep running to the bathroom. She even wears an old angora sweater under her pajamas. It's so tight and tickly it does a splendid job of keeping her awake.

74

"You're such a baby, Katie. Ten years old and scared of the dark."

"Oh, I'm scared, am I?" said Katie, and she touched the volume control on the television. She was watching one of those awful *Tales from the Crypt* movies and just the sound of the creepy music made me put my head back under the covers.

It was my friend Graham who helped me figure things out. He gets a bit bothered and fidgety if I barge into his bedroom but we sometimes have these little chats on the stairs now. He used to share a bedroom with Katie when they were both little so he knows what it's like.

"She didn't have a television then so she used to make me play all these games with her and then we'd have to take turns telling ghost stories and whenever I fell asleep she'd pinch me and once she hit me so hard with her flashlight I had a black eye in the morning *and* I got into trouble with Dad for it because he said I was a little wimp if my kid sister could get the better of me in a fight," Graham said, sighing.

"Doesn't she get tired like other people?"

"Yes, of course she does. Haven't you seen the dark circles under her eyes? And she sometimes falls asleep at school."

"So why won't she go to sleep at night like anyone else?"

"Because she's scared."

"But she *makes* herself scared, watching all those horrid videos."

"No, that's to keep her awake. She's scared of going to sleep."

"Huh?" I stared at him. "What's there to be scared of about going to sleep?"

Graham fidgeted quite a bit. He screwed up his face several times and took his glasses off and polished them.

"She's just scared, that's all."

"But what *of*?"

Graham's eyes looked very strange and bare and pink without his glasses. They blinked a lot.

"When our mom died they told us she'd gone to sleep," he said, swallowing. "Paula and I knew she'd been ill and then we knew she was dead. But Katie was just this little squirt and she didn't know what dead meant. So they said it was just like going to sleep. They meant to be kind but she got very scared of going to sleep after that."

"I *see*."

"Andy?"

"What?"

"Don't tease her about it, okay? I mean, I know

she's a real pain, she's my own sister and even I can't stand her, but all the same, don't go on about it.''

"I won't.''

And I didn't. That night I didn't even moan when she kept bumbling around the bedroom hour after hour. I settled down and went to sleep myself. I woke up about midnight. I looked over. Katie was still awake, sitting bolt upright staring at the TV screen.

"Katie.'' I reached out and touched her. She was icy cold. "Hey. Why don't you switch that off and come in my bed and cuddle, okay?''

She paused. There was a little silence. Then she gave a sniff.

"What on earth makes you think I want to come in your bed, Andy Pandy? You're so big and fat I'd get squashed flat in five minutes.''

I *still* didn't tease her. But I was dying to.

is for Old People

I don't like Old People. They really get on my nerves.

Miss Maynard is old. She's my principal. I had to go and see her the other day. She started off being quite palsy and she even offered me one of her special toffees but then she started in on me.

"It's just not good enough, Andrea. Your schoolwork's gone to pieces this year. You don't hand your homework in on time, or you don't even bother to do it. You don't have your P.E. uniform in class. You don't bring a proper sick note when you've been out of school. What's going on, mmm?"

My teeth got jammed in this huge glob of toffee so

I could only manage to urgle-urgle in response. Anyway, how could I explain properly? I'm so busy flitting from my mom's place to Dad's and back again that I leave half my stuff behind. I hand Mom my P.E. stuff to go in the wash and then I forget to take it with me to Dad's. It's no use expecting Carrie to do it. She washes but she doesn't ever iron anything and I get teased when I'm at Dad's because my school blouses are all crumpled and once they came out shocking pink because Carrie shoved my stuff in with Zen's scarlet sweater. Carrie didn't even say she was sorry. She said she thought the pink shirt looked lovely with my bottle-green uniform, much better than boring old white.

I don't always bring a sick note because I forget to ask Mom or Dad . . . and maybe just occasionally I'm not exactly sick, I'm just staying out of school because I'm fed up with it. No one knows. I pretend to Mom or Dad that I'm going to school and I get on all the right buses but I don't always get off in the right place. I wander around town instead. Sometimes I go to the garden on Larkspur Lane and Radish and I spend hours and hours there. She sails backward and forward across the lake and then she hikes through the jungle or climbs the north face of Mount Mulberry . . .

"Andrea!" Miss Maynard put her thin wrinkly face

close to mine. "You've gone off into a daydream! For goodness' sake, girl, you must stop this silly habit. I know things have been difficult for you at home."

"I haven't *got* a home anymore. Mom and Dad—"

"Yes, I know. And I do sympathize. But I can't help thinking you're making a rather unnecessary fuss. You know as well as I do that lots and lots of parents divorce and move to new houses. It's very upsetting, but it's not the end of the world. We've been making allowances for you long enough, Andrea. Now it's time you started pulling yourself together."

She gave my shoulders a little shake as if she was really pulling me together. I felt that if she went on pulling I'd go *twang* like elastic.

Mr. Roberts is old too. Really old, with white hair and a beard, but he still works the counter in his candy store though he can't bend anymore because he says his knees are gone. You can't see whether they really are gone or not because of his corduroy pants. Bill the baboon doles out pocket money on Saturdays. I get it too when I'm around, and then we all go down the road to the neighborhood stores. Paula's always worrying about her figure so she doesn't go to Mr. Roberts's candy store, she buys tapes and magazines from the newsstand on the corner. Graham and Katie and I go to the candy store.

"Hello, my darlings," Mr. Roberts says as soon as

he sees us. He's always twinkling and stroking his beard. You expect him to go Ho-ho-ho like Santa Claus.

Graham is very shy with most people but he gets quite talkative with Mr. Roberts. But it's Katie who is the favorite. Naturally. She twirls around the shop like a sugarplum fairy and Mr. Roberts chuckles and claps and calls her his Little Precious and his Cute Little Sweetheart. He always lets her have a free pick from his Lucky Bag, five cents a dip.

He offers me a free pick too but I just stick my nose in the air and say no thanks. I have to buy my candy and chocolate from him because there's nowhere else to get it, but I'm not going to make friends.

Mr. Roberts and I are deadly enemies. The very first time I went into his shop with Graham and Katie he looked me up and down and then he whispered to Katie, "Who's the Jolly Green Giant?"

It was a loud whisper and I heard. Katie sniggered and snorted and even Graham smiled. He said later that Mr. Roberts just called me that because I was wearing my green school raincoat. Rubbish. It was a studied insult because of my size.

The grannies and granddads are all old too. I can't stand any of them. I have my own Nan and Grand-dad but they live in Canada with my auntie so they're no use. They're Dad's mom and dad. Mom's mom and dad are dead so they're no use either. It's not fair, because Paula and Graham and Katie have two full sets of grandparents and they're always coming to see them, and Zen and Crystal have a granny and grandpa too. *They* aren't too bad, because they took me to the zoo with them, and we all got ice cream and an animal coloring book. Paula and Graham and Katie's are awful. The baboon's parents are squat and hairy like him, even the granny. I'd hate to kiss her because she has a mustache. But the worst ones of all are the other gran and granddad. They used to help look after Paula and Graham and Katie after their mom died. They still come and visit a lot. They don't think much of my mom. They keep going on about the past, and how devoted Bill was to his first wife, and Mom gets very pink in the face. They practically ignore her. And me. You will never believe this but when they come on a visit they always bring presents for Paula and Graham and Katie. Sometimes they're really big presents, new clothes or books or records. Sometimes it's just boxes of chocolates. But whatever it is, I don't get anything at all. Not a crumb.

Mom got pinker than ever, pinker than my spoiled school shirts, and eventually I heard her ask the gran and granddad if they could include me in the present-giving so that I wouldn't feel left out.

"But Paula and Graham and Katie are our grandchildren," they said. "Andrea has nothing to do with us."

Well, good. You won't catch *me* wanting to have anything to do with *them*.

is for Photographs

Dad's got a camera. We're back to the old routine now. One week at Mom's. One week at Dad's. You know. As easy as ABC. Carrie was a bit huffy at first because she'd had a social worker come around to check up on things.

"And she said everywhere is spotless," said Carrie. "You tell your mother that. We might be a bit untidy, but the apartment is perfectly clean and she said that Zen and Crystal are delightful intelligent children who have obviously had a lot of loving care and stimulation."

The delightful and intelligent twins were having a

fierce pillow fight as she spoke, lovingly and carefully stimulating the pillows until they both burst simultaneously and scattered a snow of feathers.

Carrie just laughed. Even Dad didn't get mad. He got his camera and took lots of photos.

"You'll wear that camera out before the baby's even born," said Carrie, still laughing. She turned to me. "I bought your dad this secondhand camera so he can take lots of photos when the baby's being born. Won't that be lovely?"

I stared at her. I know how babies are born, of course. I didn't think they were going to be the sort of photos you could put in a silver frame and prop on top of the television set.

Dad saw me looking doubtful.

"I want to take lots of photos of my number one daughter too," he said. "Come on, Andy, give me a smile."

I gave him a smile. And then another. And then I put my hand on my hip and gave him a little wave. Then I pointed a toe. Then I pirouetted around the room, Dad going *snap snap snap*.

"Attagirl, Andy. Hey, that's great. You've really got the idea, haven't you?"

It was wonderful. I felt like a film star. Crystal came and joined in and she smiled and waved and pointed too, but she didn't do it as naturally as me. And Zen was hopeless, galumphing around and making hideous faces at the camera.

"No, Andy's the star model," said Carrie. "Here, let's dress her up like a real model, okay? Come and help me choose some clothes, Crystal. And we'll make her up and give her a glamorous hairdo. Would you like that, Andy?"

I liked it enormously. Carrie dressed me up in one of her long droopy fancy dresses and Crystal draped a shawl around my shoulders and stuck a ring on every finger. Carrie stroked dark shadow on my eyelids and purple lipstick around my mouth and then brushed my hair up into a crazy kind of bun. Crystal squirted me all over with perfume even though it wouldn't show in a photograph.

Then we had a long, long posing session, Dad snapping away until he eventually ran out of film. He developed the photographs himself, blundering around in the bathroom in the pitch dark. I couldn't wait to see the finished photographs. I felt as if I'd been transformed into this new grown-up magical pretty person. I looked for her in the photographs—but I just saw myself, looking a bit funny in a long dress with stuff smeared all over my face.

"I don't like them. Tear them up, Dad. Ugh, I look awful," I said hastily.

"No, they're very good. The lighting's a bit hay-wire and you're out of focus here and there, but on the whole they're great," said Dad.

"*You* look great, Andy," said Carrie. "You know what? You'll have to be a fashion model when you grow up. You're nice and tall already. Fashion models have to be very tall."

I didn't know that. I thought about the idea. Maybe the photographs weren't too bad after all.

Dad gave me some copies to show to Mom when it was her turn to have me.

"Oh, for Heaven's sake!" said Mom. "Look at the way they've dressed you up! You look awful, Andy. All that dreadful makeup. And you're wearing that Carrie's clothes. Why on earth couldn't your father take some good photos of you in your own clothes, in-stead of all dolled up like a dog's dinner?"

"I was being a fashion model, Mom. Carrie said I could be a model when I grow up, she did, Mom, honestly."

"She would," said Mom, shuddering.

"Fashion models aren't *fat*," said Katie, poking me in the tummy.

"I can go on a diet when I grow up," I said, but I was starting to wish I hadn't taken the photos with me.

But then Paula came and had a look.

87

"Don't you look grown-up, Andy? No one would ever think you were only ten. You look almost as old as me."

That pleased me quite a lot.

And then Graham had a quick shuffle through the photos too.

"Don't, Graham. I look like such a flake," I said, getting steamed.

"Yeah, you said it, Andy Pandy," said Katie.

"I think you look pretty," said Graham.

That pleased me even more.

is for Questions

"What's Miss Maynard talking about in this letter, Andy? She's moaning about all your dental appointments, saying it would be better if you could go after school. But you haven't *had* any dental appointments, have you? You went for a checkup in the summer and you didn't even need any fillings. So what's going on, Andy? *Andy?*"

"How did you do on your English test, Andy? And how's the old arithmetic getting on? Why won't you let me see your schoolbooks nowadays? You're still at the top of the class, aren't you? Andy, what's the matter?"

"Come along, Andrea, answer the question. It's no use looking at Aileen, she's not going to tell you. You weren't paying attention, were you? It's simply not good enough. Do you want to end up a complete dunce, is that it?"

"Who's been fooling around with my pantyhose? They're all wet and soapy. You've been messing around with your little rabbit again, haven't you?"

"How are things working out for you and Radish, Andrea? Do you mind going from House A to House B and back again?"

"Do you know what time it is, Andy Pandy? Time to go home. Only you haven't got a home anymore, have you?"

is for Radish

I didn't dare skip school for a while because Mom went to see Miss Maynard and they had a Long Talk. I'm never going to be able to pretend I've got to go to the dentist now even if I get a gum infection and half my fillings fall out. I can't even get a cold or a cough or a tummy upset. Miss Maynard showed Mom my forged sick notes. And then Mom told Dad so I won't even be able to swing things when I'm at his place. I have to stay at boring old school even though the teachers just shout at me now and Aileen and Fiona whisper secrets and won't play with me and I keep coming out at the bottom on all the tests.

I can't even go to the garden for long after school because Mom knows what time I should get back to her place and even though she's not there Katie always tells on me. It's even worse when I'm at Dad's. Carrie comes to meet me off the bus and she looks awful now with her big huge bump and I'm scared people will think she's a real relative instead of just a stupid stepmother. I just have time to charge down Larkspur Lane, climb over the gate, give Radish one quick sail across the lake and back, maybe let her take a two-minute hike in the grassy jungle, and then it's home again home again *jiggety jig* only I haven't got a home anymore and Radish seems to be getting a bit fed up with my pocket.

I wish I could make a real home for her. I tried making her a Japanese bag out of one of Dad's hankies and then I thought about making her a real little Japanese house but Crystal kept trailing around after me asking what I was doing, and then when I got the big box of kitchen matches to construct a wooden house Carrie suddenly swooped and snatched them away.

"I'm sorry, Andy, but I can't let you play with matches."

"I'm not going to *play* with them. I'm going to make something with them."

"Yes, it's going to be a little house and she's made

92

a tiny screen out of a cigarette package and a baby tree out of a twig and she's going to make Radish a special dress called a kimono," Crystal burbled.

"Shut *up*, Crystal," I hissed, because it would all get spoiled if everyone knew.

It was spoiled anyway. Carrie still wouldn't let me have the matches. I did try to think how to make the house with something else but then Zen stepped on the screen after I'd spent ages coloring in little tiny Japanese things all over it. Carrie helped me a bit. In fact she did the drawing part and she had the ideas and Zen kept pestering and eventually he just went *stamp*. Carrie said we could do another screen but I said no thanks. I didn't really want her poking her nose in anyway. I wanted it to be a secret for Radish and me with no one else involved, not even Crystal.

I tried again when I was at Mom's. I swiped an old shoe box and I spent ages getting all the thread off some spools but Katie was poisonous.

"Oh, how sweet. Little Andy Pandy's playing house with her dinky toy rabbit. But I think it's rather a risky site. I have a feeling this is an earthquake area. What's that? Did you feel a tremor? Whoops!"

She reached out and Radish and her home went flying. So then I reached out and Katie went flying.

Mom was furious and wouldn't even listen why.

"I've told you and told you, Andy. You are *not* to

93

hit Katie, no matter what. You *must* stop this disgraceful bullying, especially when Katie's so much smaller than you.''

And as if that wasn't enough, Katie deliberately pulled two buttons off her school blouse. Mom saw and tutted and went to her sewing box—and then I got into another fight because she said I'd messed up all her thread.

I was in so much trouble that I decided I might just as well stay for ages in the Larkspur Lane garden and miss my bus. Miss two buses, even three. Katie could blab all she liked to Mom because I'd stopped caring.

"Do you hear that, Radish?" I said as we climbed over the gate. "We can stay here as long as you like."

Radish wriggled excitedly in my hand. She could hardly wait till I got her boat unpacked from my backpack. She hopped on board and was soon sailing across the lake, expertly skimming her way through the schools of orange whales. I let her sail under her own steam, squatting down on the muddy shore and watching her, but after a while it got a bit cold and damp so I found a long twiggy stick and started propelling her around the lake in uncharted territory. Together we discovered Step Creek and Lily Land and for a while we were caught up in the fetid swamps of Waterweed Bog but we escaped at last after Radish heroically hacked her way through with her bare paws and my scrabbling fingernails.

She was a bit tired of sailing after that and we'd both got very wet so we ran around and around the lake to get warm. We were hungry too and looked longingly at the mulberry tree but the berries were long since over. I searched the lining of my backpack and salvaged a few cookie crumbs but they weren't much of a feast for Radish and they didn't help my hunger at all.

I don't have a watch but I knew it was dinnertime. I was really really late now. It was starting to get dark. Mom would be back from work and she'd be so mad. She'd tell the baboon and he'd have another round with me. And Katie would give a smug little smile and then whisper about it half the night. I wouldn't even be able to cry because she'd see.

I leaned against the mulberry tree clutching Radish in my fist and had a bit of a cry there. But then as I moved around to keep my face from getting scratched, my hand holding Radish suddenly slipped under a branch and went into a little hole.

"Radish? Come back!"

But Radish was running around inside the dark little hole, getting excited. It was just like a secret cave. I tried to peer in but it was getting too dark to see well. Radish insisted that she could see. She loved the little hole. Only it wasn't a hole to her. She wanted me to help her make it into a real home. Not a real permanent home, but a vacation home for her visits to the lake.

"Okay, Radish. We'll make it really cozy for you. We could get some moss for a soft green carpet. And I could stick some shiny leaves together to make matching curtains. And we'll have to see about some sort of light because I can't see in the dark even if you can."

And at that moment a light went on. Not inside the hole. Outside. In the big house behind me. It made me jump and my hand jerked and then suddenly Radish wasn't there.

"Radish? Radish, where are you? Come back! Come here!" I said, feeling frantically. And then I felt the drop at the back of the hole. I pushed my arm in as far as it would go. I clawed and stretched but it was no use. Radish had fallen out of my reach.

"Radish!" I screamed.

And then the door opened and there was a dark figure in the garden and I had to tear my arm out of the tree and run for it.

is for Starlight

"Where on earth have you *been?*" Mom shouted.

I was too choked up to answer properly.

"I was just . . . playing," I mumbled.

"Playing!" said Mom, and she smacked me hard across the face.

We both gasped. She'd never hit me before. Then I burst into tears. And Mom did too.

"Oh, Andy," she said, and she was suddenly hugging me tight. "I'm sorry. I was just so worried and I've been phoning everyone. I phoned Miss Maynard, and I had to phone your father and he blames me for working and yet if he'd pay his share of the bills then I wouldn't have to and— Oh, darling, never mind all that. All that matters is you're safe."

"But Radish isn't," I said, and I started really howling. I'd held it in while waiting for the first bus and then on the trip and then on the second bus and then on the walk back to Mom's place but now the full awfulness washed over me like a giant wave.

"I've lost Radish," I sobbed, and I buried my head in Mom's shoulder so I could shut out all the other faces around me. Graham looked sympathetic and Paula patted my shoulder but Katie had her eyebrows raised in mock amazement and the baboon looked impatient.

"For goodness' sake, is that why she's so late? Because she's lost her little toy?" he said, sighing.

"She's *not* a toy, she's a mascot," I shouted.

"Hey, hey! No need to use that tone. Look, your poor mom's been worried sick. You're two hours late getting home, young lady. It's just not good enough."

"Yes, I know, Bill, but Radish is very special to Andy," said Mom, still holding me close.

"All the same, it seems a bit ridiculous to have the whole family acting demented because she's lost a little rabbit that isn't even real."

"She *is* real to me!"

"Come on now, Andy, calm down. You really are being a bit of a baby, you know," said Mom. She said it quietly but the others could still hear. I pulled away from her. "Andy? Now don't be like that. Look, maybe Radish isn't lost forever. When did you last see her? Did she drop out of your pocket on the way home?"

"She fell down inside a tree," I whispered, thinking of poor little Radish tumbling backward down that dark hole.

"Which tree?" said Mom, but I couldn't tell her because I'd get into more trouble for going into someone else's garden. Oh, how could I have run off like that and left my Radish down in the depths of the mulberry tree? And she wasn't the only thing I'd abandoned in my hurry to save my own skin.

"I've lost your lovely little boat too, Graham," I said, crying harder.

"Never mind. Look, I can easily make you another," Graham said gruffly.

"But there can never be another Radish," I said, sobbing.

"Of course there can," said the baboon. "I'll get you a new one in the morning. They sell them in the toy shop down the road. Katie had some of those tiny rabbit toys when she was little."

The "little" stung, but I was so overwhelmed with misery and guilt I hardly cared.

"I don't want a new rabbit. I want *Radish*."

Radish hadn't died. She hadn't stopped being. She was still there, alone in the dark tree, probably hurt, certainly very lonely and scared. She'd be wondering where on earth I was, why I wasn't coming to rescue her . . .

"I've got to go back," I said desperately. "I can't reach her, but I could call down to her, try to comfort her—"

"Don't be so silly, darling," said Mom. "You're certainly not going out again. You're going to have some dinner and a nice hot bath and then you're going straight to bed."

There was no arguing with her. There *was* a lot of arguing going on, but that was between Mom and Dad, because Dad came around to see if I was safe and then started up all the old fights. My hand kept reaching out for Radish and then clenching in despair.

It was even worse when I went to bed. I couldn't remember ever going to sleep without Radish. She was always tucked into my hand and I put my finger in between her dear little ears and rubbed her soft furry forehead until I went to sleep. So now of course I couldn't possibly sleep. I lay awake hour after hour. Mom crept in to see me and gave me a special kiss and tucked me in while Katie made vomit noises from the next bed, but it didn't help. I heard Graham go to bed. Then Paula. Then Mom and the baboon. Soon the whole household was asleep except me. And Katie. She started.

"Down a tree, is she, Andy Pandy? In with all the bugs and spiders, eh? You get lots of creepy crawlies inside trees. And maybe some bird's fallen down the hole too and died and your little Radish is lying on its *corpse.* Yeah, all the maggots are going *wiggle wiggle wiggle* all over her and she won't even be able to cry for help because rabbits don't talk. She's just opening her little mouth and screaming silently, wondering why you don't come."

"I *am* coming," I said. I got out of bed and started pulling on my clothes.

"What are you doing, you dope?" Katie whispered.

"What do you *think* I'm doing? I'm going to comfort Radish," I said, pulling on a sweater.

"But it's after midnight. You can't go *out.*"

"Just watch."

"But your mom—"

"I don't care. She won't know. And if you tell her

I'll . . . I'll tell you're such a scared baby you won't even lie down to go to sleep. And I know why and I'll tell everyone—if you tell on me. Understand?''

She understood, all right. She still looked worried.

"Andy, you are just kidding, aren't you? You can't really go out in the middle of the night. Look, those things I said about Radish, I was just making them up to annoy you, they're not true.''

"They could be," I said, and I put on my coat and wound a scarf around my neck.

"But it's so dark outside," said Katie.

She was wrong about that. When I'd crept down the stairs and out the front door I looked up and saw there was a big round moon and hundreds of stars shining in the sky. I saw the North Star shining brighter than all the others. I threw back my head, staring at it until my eyes watered, and I whispered the wishing song.

> *Starlight, star bright*
> *First star I see tonight*
> *I wish I may, I wish I might*
> *Have the wish I wish tonight.*

"I wish that I can find Radish and work out a way of reaching her so that I can have her back, please, please, *please.*"

is for Time to Go Home

There aren't any buses in the middle of the night. Larkspur Lane is a long bus ride away. I wasn't sure how long it would take me to walk. I'd never been out that late at night before. Certainly not by myself. The stars and the streetlights kept it from being too dark, but it was still pretty scary. It was cold and strange and all the streets seemed so empty, but whenever a car went by or a man walked past I shrank away from them.

I tried to think of poor little Radish stuck inside the tree—but I couldn't stop thinking about poor little *me* too. I remembered all the things Mom and Dad had said about strangers, and when a man slowed down when he saw me and said, "What's up, dear? Why are you out all on your own at this hour?" I shot past and went flying off down the street. He called after me and then started running too.

I ran faster, heart thudding, feet pounding, dodging down an alley and around someone's garden and down another passage and out onto another road and then another, running and running and running—and when at last I stopped, spread-eagled against a wall with a horrible tearing stitch in my side, the man was nowhere to be seen.

He might have been a kind man trying to look after me. He might have been a monster ready to make off with me. There was no way of telling.

I didn't even know where I was anymore. I stared around at the dark unfamiliar buildings in panic. I could try going back along the alley but the man might be waiting . . .

I started shaking and shivering. My cheeks got a bit wet. My hand seemed horribly empty—but then I tucked my thumb inside my fist and tried to kid myself it was Radish and it helped just a little bit. I ran on down the road and when I turned the corner I was at the stores. I knew how to get back to Mom's place in less than five minutes. But I couldn't go back. Katie would be still lying awake, and how she'd sneer if I came creeping back so soon. And Radish was still in the tree, so lost and lonely and frightened. I thought of her tiny heart beating violently under her soft fur and my face screwed up in pain.

"I'm coming, Radish," I whispered. I stared up at the stars. "You've *got* to make my wish come true."

So I started walking. I walked and walked and walked. I walked until I was so tired I started to wonder if I was dreaming. Everything seemed so strange and silvery in the starlight and every so often my head would nod and I'd stumble and start. I kept expecting to blink and find myself tucked into bed at Mom's, but it didn't happen. So I just walked some more, my head down, shoulders hunched, feet going *left right left right left right.*

I lost my way several times but then I'd suddenly recognize a store or a house and I'd know I was back on course again. But then I found myself in streets I was certain I'd never seen before. I walked on and yet it was all new and different and I realized I was lost again. I tried going back but I kept getting to corners and not knowing whether to turn left or right. So in the end I kept on walking anyway, and after a while I stopped thinking about finding the way. I just looked up at the stars and whispered Radish's name and walked on and on and on.

Then I suddenly recognized a house at the end of a road, with gables and a curly iron gate and an RV parked in the front drive. It was Aileen's house and she went on her vacations in that RV and we'd swung on that gate together and she was probably asleep in her bedroom under the gables right this minute.

"Aileen's house?" I whispered. Then I'd somehow missed Larkspur Lane altogether. I'd bypassed the school. I was back in my own old territory, the other side of the school. The part of town where I never went anymore. If this was Aileen's house then I knew what was down the road and around the corner.

I stood still, shivering. No. I had to go to Larkspur Lane and find Radish. I couldn't waste time going anywhere else. But I had to. My feet started walking and I couldn't stop them.

I went past Aileen's house. Past all the other houses on the road with their neat privet hedges and their pointed roofs making a zigzag pattern against the starry sky. I got to the corner. I stood still again, holding my thumb. Then I started walking, very very slowly.

I could see it in the starlight. A cottage at the end of the road. I could only see in black and white but it was easy to paint in the colors. A white cottage with a gray slate roof and a black chimney and a bright butter-yellow front door. There were yellow roses and honeysuckle growing up a trellis around the door and the leaded windows, and lots of other flowers growing in the big garden. And in the middle of the garden was the old twisted tree with the big branches bent almost to the ground, and at the tip of each twig grew big bunches of black mulberries . . .

No, no mulberries. The berries had long ago withered on the tree. No roses, just tangled thorny branches. No sweet-smelling honeysuckle, just leathery stems trailing untidily. But it was still Mulberry Cottage. I was back. I was home.

is for Unconscious

"Andy? Andy darling, is that you?" Mom's at the door, smiling at me. "Come in, sugar-lump, I've got tea all ready on the table."

"Yes, come on, Andy, Mom's made a lovely mulberry pie and my mouth's watering," Dad calls.

"Dad?" I step inside, shaking my head. "Dad, what are you doing here?"

"He got off work early, didn't you, darling," says Mom.

"But what are *we* doing here?" I say, dazed.

"We live here, silly," says Mom, and she ruffles my hair. "What's up, Andy? Don't you feel very well?"

"No, I feel . . . wonderful. I can't believe it. Was

it all a dream, then—all that about leaving Mulberry Cottage and you having Bill and Dad having Carrie and . . . ?"

"I think you're still half asleep, dear. Come on, let's have tea, we're all hungry."

Mom takes my hand and leads me into the living room. Dad's sitting at the table, smiling at me. There's a big bunch of our own pink roses in a pretty white vase, and there are little cupcakes with pink icing and white rosettes and the newly baked mulberry pie, dark wine-red juice bubbling up through a crack in the golden pastry and filling the whole room with the rich fruity smell.

Mom cuts me a huge slice and tops it with vanilla ice cream. I bite into hot and cold, crunchy and smooth, sweet and sharp, and close my eyes with the bliss of it.

"Mmmmm," I say, and Mom and Dad laugh.

"Doesn't Radish want some too?" says Mom.

"Radish?" I say, and there she is, safc and sound, tucked into my pocket, half asleep too.

Mom lets me fetch a doll's house saucer and a china thimble and Radish eats and drinks with us.

"But wait. This is the thimble I swapped with Aileen ages ago," I say, puzzled.

"Well, you must have swapped it back again," says Mom.

"And maybe you'll be swapping yet again because I've got a little surprise in my pocket for you and your Radish," says Dad.

"A present!" I jump up and run to Dad.

"Oh, darling, you do spoil her," says Mom.

"I like spoiling both my best girls," says Dad, and he gives me a present out of one pocket and Mom a present from the other.

Mine is a small square cardboard box and inside are a tiny Radish-size gilt table and chair, and Scotch-taped safely to the tabletop are a tiny pink china cup and saucer and plate, delicately edged with a wisp of gold paint. Mom's present is in another cardboard box and it's a full-size pink china teacup and saucer with cherubs flying all around the rim, and a little message in looping writing at the bottom of the cup. The message says "I love you." Dad says it too. Mom goes as pink as her cup and they give each other a long kiss. Radish and I grin at each other. We are all very pleased with our presents.

We eat up the pie and ice cream and every one of the cupcakes and then we all wash the dishes together, making it a game. Dad keeps flapping the dishtowel and I put my fingers on my head to make horns and rush around pretending to be a little bull and Mom makes like we're getting on her nerves but she keeps laughing, and we're still all in a giggly mood when we go back into the living room, as if it's a special day like Christmas.

We switch on the television and my very favorite movie, *The Wizard of Oz,* is just starting and so Mom and Dad and Radish and I all cuddle up to watch it. I've got my red slippers on and Mom and Dad keep calling me Dorothy and I turn Radish into Toto and make her give little barks. We sing along to all the songs and at the end of the movie when Dorothy clicks the heels of her ruby slippers and whispers, "There's no place like home," I suddenly start crying.

"What's up, darling?" says Mom.

"Don't be sad, little honeybunch," says Dad.

"I'm not sad. I'm crying because I'm so happy," I say, sniffling.

"You funny old thing," says Mom, and she pulls me onto her lap to cuddle.

When the movie ends I climb onto Dad's lap instead and he reads me a story, lots of stories, from all the storybooks I had when I was little.

"But they got lost somewhere, I'm sure they did," I say.

"Well, we found them again, especially for you," says Dad, giving me a kiss.

"You don't mind reading me such babyish stuff, Dad?"

"You're our baby, aren't you?" says Dad, giving me a tickle. "Come on, little babykins, say *cootchy-coo* for your Dad-Dad."

"Oh, Dad, don't be so silly," I say, shrieking with laughter.

"I don't know—tears one minute, a great big fit of the giggles the next. I think it must be bedtime," says Mom.

"Oh no," I say, but I don't argue too much because I don't want to spoil anything and it's easy to be good when I'm so happy. I get into the bathtub and Radish gets in with me and floats around as merry as a little duck. Then we both get dry and powdered and into our nighties and then Dad comes and carries me into bed as if I really am a baby. He tucks me in and he tucks Radish in too, and he kisses both our noses, which makes me giggle again. Then Mom comes and she tickles us both under the chin and we giggle some more. Then Mom and Dad stand arm in arm at the foot of my bed, chatting softly to each other while Radish and I snuggle up. The bed's so soft and I feel so safe with all my own things around me, my own rabbit pictures on the wall, my own wardrobe, my own toy cupboard, my own bookshelf, my own Radish in my hand, my own Mom and Dad right by my bed, together. I'm so happy I want this moment to last forever but I'm so sleepy too and

I can't stop my eyes closing and I know I'm going to sleep and I'm suddenly worried because I know it can't last and that it's going to be very different when I wake up and I try to open my eyes wide but they're so heavy and I have to rest them just for a second and then they won't open again and I'm going to sleep in spite of myself, I'm going to sleep . . .

is for Vagrant

I woke up and it was dark and I was so cold and I felt for Radish but I couldn't find her and then I remembered and I couldn't bear it and I huddled under an old sack at the end of the garden and tried to get back into the dream . . .

And then I woke up again and it was light and I heard someone out in the garden, over by the bird feeder.

"Come on, little sparrows, nice toast crumbs for breakfast. Come and have a little peck. And I've got some nuts for you too and— Oh my goodness! Harry, come quick! There's some little old vagrant sleeping under the mulberry tree!"

114

A vagrant. For a moment I thought she meant a real vagrant sleeping somewhere beside me. And then I realized. She meant me.

Vagrants rough it. They don't have their own bed. They don't have a real home. Nobody wants them. They keep shifting around and getting moved on and everyone acts like they're a general nuisance.

I'm a vagrant.

I scrambled out of the old sack and struggled to my feet, and then I started running, staggering once or twice because I was so stiff. The woman gasped and then called after me but I wouldn't stop. I couldn't get the gate open so I jumped right over it. They'd painted it green instead of black. And when I risked one last look around I saw they'd painted the front door green too. It didn't look like my Mulberry Cottage without a butter-yellow front door. But it isn't my Mulberry Cottage anymore.

I ran away, stumbling down the road, around corners, along lanes, no longer watching where I was going, not even knowing anymore, just wanting to run and run. I ran right across the road and a car honked at me and made me jump so I didn't cross any more roads for a bit and then another car honked and I blinked at it, bewildered because I was still safely on the sidewalk, and it honked again and someone shouted and I saw it was Dad. Only maybe I was still dreaming because Mom was with him too, Mom and Dad together in our car, and they stopped the car with a squeal of brakes and then they were both running toward me—and suddenly I was swept up in their arms and we were having a big hug together, Mom and Dad and me, hugging the way we used to, the three of us together. No, we used to be four. Radish!

"Oh, Andy, darling, don't cry! It's all right, you're safe and we've got you back and—"

"And half the police in the country are out looking for you but we found you ourselves and just as long as you're okay—"

"Oh, Andy, why did you run away? We've been so *worried*—"

"We've been going out of our minds. Everyone's been searching—"

I cried harder. "I haven't been searching. I just gave up. And she'll be so scared without me," I sobbed. "Oh, I've *got* to go and rescue Radish!"

"But you dropped her down some tree, darling, you said—"

"I know which tree. It's in a garden where I go a lot."

"You don't mean . . . our old garden? At Mulberry Cottage?"

"No, this is a different garden. On Larkspur

116

Lane, near my school. I was looking for it last night but I got lost and then I was back at Mulberry Cottage and you were there, both of you were, and we all had tea together and then you both put me to bed—"

"That must have been a dream, Andy."

"Yes, I know. It wasn't ever like that, even before you split up," I say sadly. "But Radish isn't a dream. She really is in the tree and I have to go and try to get her back."

"That darn rabbit," said Dad, only he didn't say darn. But he drove us in the car to Larkspur Lane and I pointed out the right cottage.

"It's still very early. We can't just barge into a private garden and start searching their trees," said Mom. "Maybe we ought to wait awhile, Andy. You're still frozen stiff. We ought to take you straight back home and—"

"And we've got to phone the police, tell them you're safe."

"And I must let Bill and the children know. They're all so worried. Katie's been in floods of tears."

"*Katie?*"

"Carrie and the twins are very upset too—and it's bad for Carrie to get in a state when the baby's nearly due."

117

"But I've *got* to get Radish," I said, starting to climb over the gate.

I was up and over the other side before they could stop me.

"Andy, come back!"

"We must knock at the front door first to ask permission."

"No, we can't. I'll get into trouble," I whispered, running across the wet grass toward the mulberry tree. "It's okay, I know exactly where Radish is, and if you could try to get your arm down the hole, Dad, you can reach much farther than me—"

But before I could get to the tree I heard the door of the house opening, and someone coming out. Two people. They'd caught us.

is for Welcome

They were two small plump elderly people, both in their bathrobes. The woman was wearing a pink quilted satin affair, the man a woolen red-and-blue tartan job. They both had those old-fashioned slippers with pompoms. They certainly didn't look very frightening but I was in such a silly state I was frightened all the same.

"Please. I just want to look for Radish. I—I'll only be a moment," I stammered.

"We're so sorry to disturb you like this," said Mom.

"I know she's very naughty for playing in your garden, but my daughter's lost her toy rabbit in your tree and that's why we're here at this godforsaken hour, you see, to try to find it," said Dad.

"Oh, it's perfectly all right. We were expecting you," said the old man.

"Expecting the little girl. She's our little visitor," said the old woman. "She comes nearly every day and we're always so pleased to see her."

I blinked at them in astonishment.

"It's been grand to see her enjoying our garden. All our grandchildren are in Australia so we've no children of our own to come and play," said the old man.

"Of course we didn't like to intrude. We've been careful to keep our distance, but we couldn't help having little peeks at you now and then," said the old woman, smiling at me. "You and your little rabbit seemed to be having such fun. And yesterday you stayed such a long time and it was such a pleasure to us. But it started to get dark and we wondered if you might have lost track of the time. We hoped you might come indoors and take a bite of supper with us but when I came out to ask I must have startled you, because you ran away."

"I'm sorry," I said, blushing. "That was silly. And I left Radish. I dropped her down inside the mulberry tree. Do you mind if my dad tries to get her back?"

"Not at all, my dear, not at all. Although you can

120

easily reach her yourself, you know," said the old man, and he gave his wife a little nudge.

"Why don't you go and look," she said, her eyes twinkling.

So I ran to the mulberry tree. I found the little hole under the branch. But it wasn't just a hole anymore. Someone had stuck some little net curtains up at the entrance, turning it into a tiny window. I peered inside—but I couldn't see Radish.

"That's upstairs," said the old woman. "I think she's downstairs now."

I put my hand in the hole and felt, but the old woman was shaking her head.

"No, dear, there's a much easier way to see downstairs. Run around to the other side of the tree and crouch down just a little," she said.

I ran. I crouched. I saw another hole in the tree. There was a small doll-size doormat at the edge, with WELCOME in very tiny cross-stitch. I peeked past the mat and there was my own darling Radish stretched out happily on her own little wooden sofa, her head propped on a blue velvet cushion.

I gazed at her until my eyes blurred.

"How did . . . ?" I whispered.

"Just our little bit of fun, my dear," said the old woman, putting her soft hand on my shoulder. "My daughter used to play games with her little dolls in-

121

side the old mulberry, turning it into a real tree house. Arthur and I were sure you'd be back so he did a bit of whittling and made the sofa and I did a bit of stitching to make the hole look a bit homey."

"It looks very very homey," I said. "And do you know what it's called? It's Radish's own Mulberry Cottage."

We all went inside the couple's own cottage because they were starting to shiver in their bathrobes and we all had tea and hot buttered toast and Mom and Dad explained about our own Mulberry Cottage and it was all so cozy and everyone was chatting away so happily that I started to wonder if my dream might really come true . . .

But then when we were back in Dad's car he started blaming Mom for not looking after me properly when I was in bed and she got furious and started in about my not even having a real bed at Dad's place and I clutched Radish and realized that some dreams can never come true.

Radish still lives with me in my pocket most of the time because I need her so much. But she has her own Mulberry Cottage too and now, nearly every day after school, I take her there. She goes boating on her lake and then she has an acorn cup of mulberry juice in her own little cottage while I have cocoa and poppy-seed cake with Mr. and Mrs. Peters. That's the name of the old couple. They asked if I'd like to call them Uncle Arthur and Auntie Gladys but I've got too many uncles and aunties already. Sometimes, just in my head, I call them Granny and Granddad. I never thought I'd like any old people. Mr. and Mrs. Peters are very old, but I like them ever so much.

is for Xmas

Y ou should have seen Mulberry Cottage at Christmas. I dipped a pinecone in green paint and then I glued on little red berries and gold stars so that Radish had her very own Christmas tree. I even made her a teeny-weeny paper chain though Mrs. Peters had to help me because I just kept tearing it. Mrs. Peters's hands are like little claws because she has arthritis but she can still make them move like magic.

She gave me my own sewing box for Christmas. It's got all these little compartments stuffed with threads and needles and a silver thimble and a tape measure that snaps back into place when you touch the button. The compartment tray lifts out and at the bottom are all sorts of materials from her own scrap bag, soft silks and velvets and different cottons with tiny sprigs of flowers and minute checks and pinhead dots, all perfect for making into dresses for Radish. She's got so many little outfits now she wants me to change her all day long so that she can show them all off.

I've made her a ballgown that covers her paws, a velvet cloak lined with cotton-ball fur, even a little sailor suit with a big white collar and a white cap with special ear holes. Mrs. Peters had to help quite a lot with that little outfit, but I did all the designing. Maybe I won't be a fashion model after all. Maybe I'll be a fashion designer. Then I don't have to worry about getting thin. Mrs. Peters is such a good cook that I'm getting bigger than ever. She doesn't mind. She says I'm a growing girl and I should eat my fill. I told Katie and she said yes, I was growing, all right, growing gi-normous, and she puffed out her cheeks and strutted around pretending to be me. People laughed and I wanted to cry but I didn't. I didn't hit Katie either. I just made out I didn't care and said I'd sooner be gi-normous than a silly little squirt like her, and went on with my sewing.

Mr. Peters gave me a whole set of wooden furniture to go in Mulberry Cottage. There's a big wardrobe that really opens, and a wonderful wooden trunk so Radish has plenty of space to store her magnificent new ensembles. Mr. Peters also gave me my own big penknife with a pearl handle, so I can do a bit of whittling myself. Mom panicked and asked Mr. Peters to look after the knife for me, so I can only whittle when I'm with him. I think Mom worried that I might run amok and stick my penknife straight into Katie. I must admit it's a tempting thought. No, I'm joking, don't worry. Katie's still foul most of the time but just occasionally she's not too bad.

She gave me a little plaster ornament of Andy Pandy for my Christmas present and I was not particularly amused, especially as I'd sewn her a special velvet hairband to tie back her lovely long hair. But then she cleared her stuff off half the windowsill and said it was mine now, and I could keep my Andy Pandy ornament there. So now I own half the windowsill and Mom found the box with some of my old stuff from our Mulberry Cottage and I've got my china rabbits and a Santa Claus in a glass snowstorm to keep Andy Pandy company, and all my books and some old photos of Mom and Dad and me back at Mulberry Cottage. Dad took a special flash photo of Radish in her Mulberry Cottage and I've got that too, and Radish has her own copy hanging on her wall like a big poster.

I gave Mr. and Mrs. Peters one of the fashion-modelly photos of me for a Christmas present. I wasn't sure they'd like it but they put it in a special silver frame and I'm in the middle of their mantelpiece with their grandchildren on either side of me.

is for Yacht

My second-best Christmas present was from Graham. I bet you can guess what it is. It begins with Y. Not a yak. A yacht. A wonderful, magnificent, correct in every detail Bunny boat for Radish.

Mr. Peters helped Graham make it. Mr. Peters saw Radish sailing in Graham's first little boat and wondered if I'd made it myself.

"You've done quite a professional little job there, Andy. You've got quite a way with wood," he said, turning the boat backward and forward admiringly (but making Radish feel terribly seasick in the process).

"Not me. Graham made it for me. He's my sort-of brother," I said proudly.

"I thought you always moaned about all these sisters and brothers of yours," said Mr. Peters.

"Not Graham. We're friends, Graham and me."

"That's good. Well, anytime you want to bring him along with you he'd be very welcome. Some Saturday, say?"

"Oh. Well. He's got lots of homework to do. And he shuts himself up with his computer for hours. I'm not sure he could spare the time," I said.

Mr. Peters just nodded. He didn't seem to mind either way. But I did.

I wanted to keep Mr. and Mrs. Peters all to myself. They'd become my sort-of grandparents and I didn't see why I should have to share them. It was enough of a pain having to share my mom and my dad.

But I liked Graham a lot. He wasn't busy *all* the time on Saturdays. He'd like to see Radish sailing his boat on the pond. He'd like Mrs. Peters and her poppy-seed cake. He'd especially like Mr. Peters and the little lean-to at the back of the house where he did his woodwork.

But what if it all got spoiled? What if Mr. and Mrs. Peters fussed over Graham, and I got left out again?

But what if it was fun? I could show Graham all my secret places in the garden and all the special things

Mr. and Mrs. Peters had made for me and Radish, and maybe they'd fuss over me a bit while he was there so he could see they liked me a lot. And maybe Graham could do some whittling with Mr. Peters while I did some sewing with Mrs. Peters and then we could all get together for tea and cakes and that way no one would be left out.

I stayed awake even longer than Katie trying to sort it all out in my head. (There was no question of asking Katie. No way. Never.)

But the next morning I waylaid Graham on the stairs and asked him over to the Peterses' place on Saturday.

"Oh, I'm not sure I could make it. I've got lots to do. No, thanks, Andy, but I'd rather not," he gabbled.

I was mad. I thought he'd be thrilled to bits. Well, *grateful* at the very least. But it turned out I had to go down on my knees and beg before he'd agree to go with me. And even then he moaned and groaned all the way.

"This is crazy, Andy. They're your friends, not mine. This old man won't really want to meet me. And I wish you hadn't shown him that boat. It was just these bits of old wood nailed together. I made it too quickly, it wasn't any good at all."

"Well, Mr. Peters thought it was *very* good. He's dying to meet you, Graham. He wants to show you all his woodwork stuff and you can try making something together."

"I can't do things with anyone watching. I'm all fingers and thumbs. Dad says I'm useless. Oh, Andy, why can't you mind your own business?" said Graham, giving me a shove.

But I didn't shove back. I understood. No wonder Graham was a bit of a wimp. Anyone would be, with the baboon for their dad. I suppose he loved Graham but he certainly didn't seem to like him. He was always nagging at him to act like a *real boy*. If the baboon was an example of a *real man* then they're a pretty sad species. My mom is *crazy* wanting a guy like the baboon. Crazy crazy crazy. Still, I don't suppose there's any way I can like it so I'll just have to lump it. Even though un-Uncle Bill is the lumpiest lump ever.

"It's okay, Graham," I said. "You don't have to feel shy. Mr. Peters is really nice and he never ever shouts or gets annoyed."

"I don't feel a bit shy," said Graham fiercely, turning red.

He got even redder when he met the Peterses. He hung his head and didn't say anything and when Mr.

Peters asked if he'd like to see all his woodwork things Graham just shrugged and didn't look interested. But it was all right after all. Mr. Peters nodded and didn't make a big deal about it and talked to me instead and Mrs. Peters talked to me too and Graham just sat and fidgeted in the armchair, but gradually his face went back to its usual pale creamy color and his hand crept out to touch the smooth wooden fruit bowl by his side.

"Take an apple, dearie," said Mrs. Peters, but he wasn't interested in the apples, he was looking to see how the bowl was made. And then he tiptoed over to the sideboard to have a good look at the fancy fretwork and Mr. Peters went to stand beside him and they started chatting. Graham didn't say much more than yes and no at first but eventually he started asking all sorts of questions and they ambled off to the lean-to together—and that was that. We practically had to drag them away when it was dinnertime, even though Mrs. Peters had made an apple tart and iced cupcakes as well as her famous poppy-seed cake.

Graham came with me to the Peterses' every second Saturday after that. He sometimes came over the Saturdays I was staying at my dad's too. He and Mr. Peters worked together on his Christmas present to me. My magnificent yacht. Radish can sail across her

132

lake in seconds now. She's hankering to take to the open sea and attempt to cross the great pond in the park. She thinks her yacht is the best Christmas present ever.

Guess what *my* best Christmas present is.

is for Zoë

Carrie gave birth to my half sister a week after Christmas. She should have hurried things up a bit so that she arrived on the real present day but that's typical of Carrie, she's always late for everything.

It was my week to stay at Mom's but Dad came around and asked if he could take me to the hospital to see the new baby all the same. I thought Mom might make a fuss but she was in a good mood because un-Uncle Bill had gotten a new decorating job and they were celebrating on the sofa with drinks and chocolates and a smoochy video so Mom said yes quite happily—and she even gave Dad a little kiss on the cheek and said congratulations.

Dad looked pleased and I dared hope that they might get back together after all if they were actually kissing each other nowadays, but when I saw the way Dad kissed Carrie at the hospital I realized there are all sorts of different kisses and some mean you love someone a lot and others mean you maybe still love someone a little tiny bit but that's all.

"Yuck yuck yuck!" said Zen, who had to come to the hospital with us. "Do you have to do all that stupid slurpy kissy stuff?"

"I want to see my sister," said Crystal, jumping up and down excitedly, her hair all over her face (Dad was looking after the twins single-handedly and they both looked even more ruffled and rumpled than usual).

"Here she is," said Carrie, holding up this little bundle in a blanket.

I was all the way down at the end of the bed and couldn't see much. Just a tiny nose and a little red mouth. It opened and the new sister started making a lot of noise.

"She's saying hello," said Carrie, grinning.

"Can I hold her, oh please can I hold her?" Crystal begged.

"Maybe you're a bit little," said Dad anxiously.

"No I'm not, am I, Mom?" said Crystal, pouting.

"I think you're big enough to hold the baby—but sit on the bed and lean against me so that she can snuggle up comfortably," said Carrie, getting Crystal and the baby carefully arranged.

"Look at me, I'm holding my sister," said Crystal, her face bright pink with pleasure.

The baby's face was pink too because she was crying.

"I'm not big, I'm little, I'm a lickle wickle baby," said Zen, and he started making loud *waaa-waaa* noises, imitating the baby.

"Come here, little baby," said Carrie, and she scooped Zen up into her arms and held him as if he really was her baby again. He wriggled and protested but you could tell he liked it.

I stood watching them. Dad had his arm around Carrie, Carrie was cuddling Zen, Crystal was holding the new baby. I fidgeted in my pocket and found Radish.

Dad saw and smiled at me.

"Do you want to hold your sister too, Andy?"

"No thanks. I'm not really that interested in babies," I said, stroking Radish's ears.

"Why don't you take a turn? You might be able to make her stop crying," said Carrie.

"But there's no room on the bed."

"You're big enough to hold her properly," said Crystal enviously, and Dad handed the baby over to me.

I popped Radish back into my pocket and took hold of the baby. She was heavier than I'd thought she would be. I didn't know how to balance her at first but then her head lolled against my chest and my arms made a sort of cradle for her. She seemed to find it comfortable. She gave one last cry, several squeaks and splutters, and then quieted completely. I looked down at her. She looked up at me. She had big blue eyes but her hair wasn't fair like Carrie's and Crystal's and Zen's. She had caramel-colored curls. She was going to be dark like Dad. Muddy brown like me.

I gently touched her starfish hand and her tiny fingers closed around my thumb.

"She's holding my hand!" I whispered.

"She likes you. She's stopped crying," said Dad.

"She's so little," I said, looking at her tiny finger-nails, all so perfect in every detail.

"She's actually quite big for a baby," said Carrie. "Much longer and stronger than Zen and Crystal were at that stage. I think she's going to be tall."

"She's like me," I said.

"Well, she's your sister, so it's not really surprising," said Dad.

"Is she still going to be called Ethel?" said Carrie.

"Yuck, Ethel's a *stupid* name," said Zen.

I swallowed. I looked down at my sister.

"Yes, it is a stupid name," I said. "She's pretty. She ought to have a pretty name."

"Well, what shall it be?" said Dad. "We've already got A for Andy and C for Crystal. What about B for . . . Bella?"

"Belly Button," said Zen, sniggering.

I wasn't too keen on a B name. Dad and Carrie might keep going and have D for Dora and E for Emma and on and on all the way through the alphabet. One little half sister was fine, but I didn't want a whole crowd of them.

"What about a Z name?" I said.

"Yeah, Z's the best. Z for Zen. That's my name," said Zen, pleased.

"Z for . . . Zoë," I said.

Zoë's my special favorite sister now. She really does like me. I can nearly always make her stop crying. And I can give her a bottle and wash her in the sink and change her diaper though I'm not sure that's such a treat. Mrs. Peters is helping me make Zoë a little smock with a Z for Zoë embroidered on the front.

I'll maybe have to try to make something for Crystal too. She's my second-favorite sister and she gets fed up quite a bit of the time because she's not big enough to do lots of things for the baby. I found her all curled up and crying in the Japanese bag the other day. I let her play with Radish for a special treat and it cheered her up a lot.

Zen gets fed up too but you won't catch me letting Radish anywhere near him!

I like helping look after Zoë so much that I never really want to pack my things on Fridays when I'm at Dad's. But then when I get to Mom's I can pal around with Graham, and Paula's given me some of her old makeup though Mom says I'm nowhere near old enough to use it yet. I look super with it on, though, really grown up. Katie smeared a whole lot of makeup on too, but she just looked silly, like a little kid with face paints. Poor old Katie.

I went to see the family counseling lady the other day because she wanted to know how Radish and I were getting along.

"We're okay," I said.

ill go to your mom's house one week and
dad's house the next?" she said.

"I've got a House A and a House B *and* a House C
now," I said. "I go to Mom's House A one week and
Dad's House B the next week and I go to Mr. and
Mrs. Peters's House C nearly every day and Radish
gets to play in her own Mulberry Cottage when she's
there, although she still lives in my pocket most of
the time."

"It must take a lot of organizing," said the lady,
smiling.

"Oh, it does. But I've got it under control now," I
said, smiling back at her. "It's as easy as ABC.
Really."